Golf Course View

Lorraine M Harris

Oak Ridge Publishing
Lady Lake, FL 32158
www.oakridgepublishing.biz

Copyright 2010 by Lorraine M. Harris. All rights reserved. No part of this book may be reproduced, stored in a retrieval system or transmitted in any form or by any means without prior written permission of the publisher, except by a reviewer who may quote brief passages in review to be printed in a newspaper, magazine or journal.

This is a work of fiction. The characters, incidents, and dialogues are products of the author's imagination and are not to be construed as real. Any resemblance to actual people, living or dead is entirely coincidental.

First printing.

ISBN# 978-0-9843270-2-7
Published by Oak Ridge Publishing
www.oakridgepublishing.biz
P.O. box 682
Lady Lake, FL 32158

Printed in the United States of America

Acknowledgements

No matter who you are, nothing happens without the help of others. I continue to have a wonderful support group. First of all, I must thank my Lord and Savior for giving me the gift of writing.

Emma Cowart, a young, aspiring photographer took the photo used in creating the book cover. Emma's understanding of what was needed is clearly demonstrated by the photo she took.

Kathy DeAngelo is a wonderful poet who wrote the poem at the beginning of the book. Kathy captured the essence of what was needed in setting the stage for Golf Course View.

What I appreciate the most about both women's creativity is that they knew very little about the book's story. Yet, they both accomplished what I wanted.

When writing a book, the most difficult part is editing. Thank you, first and foremost, to my early draft readers—Gloria (Gigi) Hey and Jo Jones. During the final editing I am forever grateful to Marjorie (Marj) McEntyre. I was fortunate enough to find individuals who provided me with wonderful advice and guidance.

My sincere thanks to my wonderful, writing group, *The Write Corner*. The members are Sharon Allen, Christie Seiler Boeke, Peggy Hatfield, Angela Hauzeur, Nancy Snyder and Julie McGlone. Their continued advice and critiquing is invaluable.

Last, but certainly not least, thank you to my loyal readers. I love meeting you at book signings and book club discussions, and hearing from you via e-mail and letters.

As always, I take full responsibility for all mistakes and liberties I might have taken.

Dedications

Words can never express how much I appreciate the unconditional love, support and encouragement I receive from my husband, Lamont, and my two daughters, Nicole and Natalie. I am especially thankful for Natalie who is a great visionary with wonderful ideas, insight, and always provides candid feedback that makes me a better writer.

In life, there is always someone who reaches out and helps someone even when they don't realize that's what they are doing. Four men took the time and helped my husband. Thank you for being there for him and they know why I had to mention them. They are: Herbert (Herb) Burrell, Robert (Bob) Kitt, Lou Volpicelli and the late Frank Meisner.

Other Books by Lorraine M. Harris

Sunday Golf Series

Sunday Golf
After Bowling

Casserole Parade Series

Casserole Parade
Casserole Surprise

Others

What Would You Do?
Not the Norm, A Small Town Story
Intuition (co-author, Deborah Seibert)

To learn more about Lorraine's other books visit her website, lorrainemharris.com or one of the Internet bookstores such as www.amazon.com, www.barnesandnoble, etc.

My Golf Course View

The manicured landscapes and ensemble of trees,
beautiful birds flapping their wings in the breeze.

The day begins early about five fifteen,
with the appearance of a little light beam.
It dances across the bedroom wall,
I think of it as my wake-up call.

It's the grounds crew arriving in the dark early morn;
the job is completed just before dawn.

I go out on the lanai with my cup of caffeine,
the sights and the sounds are simply serene.

A daily reminder of why I chose a golf course view;
It's the best time of the day, when the sun makes its debut.

Before very long the first foursome lines up to start;
I can hear the sound of the noisy golf carts.

The first shot of the day is now in flight.
The golfers are excited, but the ball is nowhere in sight.

Then there is a stream of cursing people, wearing colorful garb
traipsing through the flower bed in my backyard.

The entertainment never ends, men teaching women to do what they recommend and women cackling endlessly with their society of friends.

By the end of the week I have buckets of balls,
New ones and used ones it's quite a windfall.

It's been a good day; all the windows have been spared.
I pay up the insurance just to be prepared.

Kathy DeAngelo

Prologue

The receptionist, Sandy Lowe was anxious as people gathered around her desk, demanding answers.

Questions were flying faster than she could respond. In truth, there was very little she could say that would satisfy their complaints.

The number of people entering the Florida Villages Regional Hospital was growing. With each passing minute that an individual did not see a doctor, Sandy noticed the atmosphere was changing from understanding and patience to impatience and frustration.

Despite the angry voices, Sandy reminded herself that she was the one in control. Her tone was slow, calm, and restrained.

"Sir, I understand your wife has been waiting for almost an hour to see a doctor, but...."

The man's interruption was a roar. "No, you don't understand." He slammed his hand on the desk. "My wife is getting worse and needs to see a doctor now!"

"Sir, the doctors are doing the best they can." Pleading, her voice was trembling "Please have a seat and a doctor will see your wife soon."

The man glared at Sandy. "You said that an hour ago." He ran his hand through his hair, turned and walked away from Sandy's desk.

Sandy's shoulders relaxed as she watched the man leave, but she tensed again as he turned back around.

"Oh yeah, I almost forgot. You need to send someone into the men's restroom to clean up the vomit on the floor."

A woman pushed her way closer to Sandy's desk. "While you're at it, someone needs to clean-up the women's restroom. One of the toilets is overflowing. I don't have to tell you what has spilled all over the floor."

A man's voice said, "Send someone to clean up aisle two," followed by the man chuckling. Everyone standing at Sandy's desk looked at him, but no one laughed at his comment.

Sheepishly, the man said, "I'm sorry. I was a grocery store manager and since I've retired that's the first time I've had a chance to say that." He pointed. "Over there, a man threw up and someone needs to clean it up."

Nothing Sandy said was going to satisfy their questions. She understood everyone's growing impatience and frustration and she was trying not to take anything said, personal. However, she needed a break.

Pushing her chair back, Sandy stood up and turned to leave. Her actions provoked the people standing at her desk to react with heated shouts. "You can't leave! Come back here! We want answers, now!"

Quickly, Sandy opened the door and made her escape. For a minute, she stood with her back against the closed door. When she opened her eyes, she smiled, relieved to see a friendly face. Becky Summers, a registered nurse, her friend, and roommate.

"What's wrong? You act as if you were running from someone."

Sandy pointed. "You wouldn't believe what's going on out there. I don't know how much longer I can continue smiling and being pleasant. The wait for someone to see a doctor is much longer than usual. People are losing their patience and they're angry."

Comforting Sandy, Becky put her arm around her. "I've never seen you this rattled. Usually, you handle the complainers with a smile and are able to keep everyone happy."

"Yeah, I know but today is different. I'm telling you at one point I felt like a person lost in the woods surrounded by a pack of wolves, which were ready to attack."

"I know this won't help, but take a deep breath and do the best you can. Everyone's tired and the doctors are working as fast as they can."

"I know. I needed a break and I guess I needed to vent." Sandy whispered, "Are the doctors still saying that this is a virus?"

"Well, based on the symptoms, the doctors don't know what

else to say. They're hoping it will last no more than twenty-four to seventy-two hours."

"I better get back. Thanks for listening." Before leaving, Sandy asked, "Do you have time to go to lunch?"

"Sure. What about 11:30? That way we can beat the cafeteria crowd."

"If you don't mind, I'd rather eat somewhere else." She glanced over her shoulder, lowering her voice. "So we can talk."

The women entered Cracker Barrel and placed their name on the waiting list and five minutes later, they were being seated. They couldn't believe their luck as they followed the greeter to a secluded table located in the far back corner of the restaurant.

With only an hour for lunch, they placed their drink orders and requested the lunch special, soup and salad. Once the waitress left the table, Sandy wasted no time. "Did you know that the CDC, Center for Disease Control and Prevention was contacted?"

Becky was surprised. "No, I didn't. When did this happen?"

"I'm not sure. I overheard two doctors discussing it. When they noticed me listening, they didn't say anything else."

"Well, I would say that CDC was notified just in case this becomes a health crisis. I know the doctors are saying that this is a virus, but no one can explain the hand rashes."

With the food and drinks arriving, the women fell silent. Using the fork, Becky poked at her salad, wondering if she should tell Sandy about her suspicions. Instead of being straight forward, she asked, "Have you ever seen the movie, Outbreak?"

"I don't think so." Sandy made a face. "Why?"

"Well, the movie is about a diseased monkey that infects an entire town." Becky stopped and pointed her fork at Sandy. "I don't live in The Villages, but when I've golfed with friends there, you would be surprised at the number of people that feed the monkey squirrels."

Sandy wasn't following Becky. "Are you saying that these people may have been infected by monkey squirrels?"

Becky took a sip of coffee. "They could have been. People treat these cute little animals like they're house pets, forgetting that they can carry all types of diseases."

"I agree, but I still don't see the connection."

Becky glanced over her shoulder and leaned close to Sandy and lowered her voice. "This could be the work of a Terrorist."

Sandy started laughing. "I know you're worried about this mysterious disease, but listen to yourself. First, you say the virus is somehow similar to a movie and now you're talking about Terrorists."

"Go ahead and laugh, but the government has been known to experiment on people without their knowledge, especially when introducing a new disease. That was the case in the movie, Outbreak."

"Are you serious?" From Becky's facial expression, Sandy knew she was.

"Yes, these are scary times and nothing surprises me. Besides, a retirement community is ideal for an experiment."

Sandy coughed, smothering a laugh. "Please tell me why."

Using a napkin, Becky wiped her mouth. "Most retirement communities are made up of the elderly. Considering their age and health conditions, who would question their deaths as being anything but normal? Would you?"

Before Sandy could answer Becky continued making a strong argument for her theory. "I did some research and discovered that every year, complications from the flu cause an estimated 200,000 hospitalizations and about 36,000 deaths. Does anyone question these statistics?"

Becky answered her own question. "No. According to my research, the people most likely to get sick or die from the flu are the elderly, young children and people with chronic illnesses. I believe this disease could be in the same category and no one…." She emphasized, "No one would bother to investigate the deaths associated with this so-called virus just like no one questions the large number of flu deaths."

Sandy chewed on her lower lip. "Have you shared your theory with Dan?"

"No, I haven't because he's always accusing me of having an over active imagination."

"Well, sometimes you do." Sandy rushed on. "I think with Dan being a police officer, he might find some merit in your theory. I know you got my attention."

"Maybe, but for now let's keep this between us." Becky glanced at her watch. "We better get back to the hospital."

CHAPTER 1

Nothing is perfect, but Woodward Roberts, better known as Woody gazed at the beautiful blue sky. *"This is God's creation and it can't get much better than this."*

Smiling, his mind wandered, thinking about how he and his wife, Amanda ended up buying a house with a golf course view. Mandy, the name he preferred calling his wife gave him golf lessons for his birthday. He fell in love with the game after which, he insisted they find a house on a golf course. The sound of golf carts and loud voices interrupted his thoughts.

Three golf balls rolled down the fairway and it didn't surprise Woody when the fourth golf ball landed in his yard. He left the lanai, walked over to the ball and picked it up.

"Hey, that's my ball," a man yelled.

"You're right." Woody's voice harsh. "It was your ball. If you understand the rules of golf, you know that when you hit a ball out of bounds, you should drop a ball, take a penalty and continue golfing."

The golfer flipped Woody the bird. "Jerk! You should think about living somewhere other than on the golf course."

Walking back onto the lanai, Woody's eyes met Mandy's as she stood at the open sliding glass doors. Taking a deep breath, he waited for her to reprimand him.

Instead, she shook her head, said nothing, and turned around.

"Wait, Mandy."

Amanda took a deep breath and turned back around.

With a long face, Woody tried to explain. "I know I promised to leave the golfers alone. But, it's hard to stand by and do nothing about the golfers breaking our windows and trampling the bushes and flowers. I've had enough. This is the second time this morning and I'm tired of it."

Woody searched his wife's face for some understanding. She said nothing. He fumed. "I've had it. I'm calling the police."

"And tell them what? Before Woody could respond, Amanda softened her voice, selecting her words carefully. "Woody, you golf. You know it's nearly impossible to hit a good shot every time. Even you have hit balls into people's yards."

Woody opened his mouth to dispute what she was saying, but she hurried on. "You…we bought this house for the golf course view. Don't forget that. Besides, you do have a choice. Sit on the lanai until the first tee time starts and then go inside the house. That way you don't have to deal with the balls landing in the yard and the golfers."

Rather than argue with her, Woody lowered his head. Amanda thought how his pouting lips resembled a little boy who had been chastised by his mother. She turned and walked away. This time Woody didn't bother to stop her.

Despite the point Mandy made earlier, Woody picked up the phone and called the Marion County Sheriff's Department. Rather than deal with a low level police officer, he asked to speak to the officer-in-charge.

"This is Lieutenant Wong, how may I help you?"

"My name is Woodward Roberts and I would like to make a formal complaint about people trespassing on my property."

Woody didn't want to mislead the officer and added, "Actually, the problem is golfers coming onto my property retrieving golf balls. I thought perhaps you could arrest them or give them a ticket. Better yet, is it possible just to make a citizen's arrest?"

"Mr. Roberts, I understand how you might feel, but this isn't a crime. This is a dispute between homeowners and those golfing. I suggest you try and resolve these issues between yourselves. When a window is broken, take the golfers to small claims court or hire a mediator to resolve the dispute."

Woody said nothing to Lieutenant Wong's suggestions. Hanging up the phone, Woody's heart was pounding hard against his chest. He was angrier than when he first placed the call.

"Fine, if the police won't do anything about my complaint then perhaps I'll take matters into my own hands."

CHAPTER 2

After hanging up the phone, Dan chuckled. He couldn't believe that a homeowner actually wanted the police to arrest golfers for retrieving golf balls from his property. Several sharp telephone rings interrupted Dan's thoughts.

"Hello." He gripped the phone hard when he heard the voice of Mr. Kindle, the developer.

"What's the status of the golf club burglar?"

Dan thought, "Just get right down to business. He didn't have to say hello. How are you doing?" His response was through gritted teeth. "The status is the same. I have my men on it, but we've come up with nothing."

"Well, I don't have to tell you how important it is for you to resolve this matter. I don't understand why you haven't caught these culprits. This has gone on too long and the residents want results. Do I make myself clear?"

Dan murmured. "I understand. Is there anything else?"

Mr. Kindle's words were harsh. "Just catch this person or persons before it becomes a headliner in the newspaper or reported on the nightly news."

The phone went dead and Dan exhaled noisily. He thought, "I can't control the news and what they report."

Dan understood Mr. Kindle's concern because several months ago, The Villages made the nationwide nightly news. The report was probably still fresh in his mind. A doctor stated that The Villages was the fastest growing community with sexually transmitted diseases. By the time the doctor retracted the original statement, the damage had been done and the media exposure had affected home sales. Mr. Kindle didn't want the possibility of the golf club thievery story to have the same effect.

Serving and protecting senior citizens was different than when Dan was on the Orlando police force. Usually, the crime, their demands and concerns were petty in nature.

The Villages covered three counties, Lake, Marion, and

Sumter, but it was not a city. The population was an estimated 70,000 with the average age probably 70. For the size of the community the crime level was almost nonexistent. Instead of murders and bank robberies, the offenses consisted of speeding tickets, individuals driving under the influence, house invasions, and an occasional domestic assault.

Dan did not kid himself. He might be paid by Marion County, but he answered to the developer who was wealthy and controlled what went on in The Villages. He expected people to respond to him as if he were a city mayor.

Mr. Kindle's subtle message was loud and clear and Dan understood it. Solve the problem if you want to keep your job.

CHAPTER 3

Paul Collins who lived in The Villages and his guest, Lenny Harper had been paired with two men they didn't know. Until the eighth hole on the Nancy Lopez Golf Course, the men had been golfing at a good clip.

With everyone having to hit over water, a bottleneck had been created. The men climbed out of their golf carts and looked down the fairway. Since they couldn't tee off, they chatted about the missed and made pars and birdies.

The last two golfers in front of them were finally at the two hundred and fifty yard marker. Since Lenny was capable of hitting that distance, he was teeing off last.

When everyone finished, Lenny stepped up to the tee box. Taking several practice swings, he swung his driver back and forth. Addressing the ball, Lenny's club made contact and all eyes turned upward.

One man cupped his hand over his eyes, watching the soaring ball. "Man, I lost your ball, it went too high and the bright sun rays blinded my vision. I have no idea where it landed."

Lenny pointed. "I think I hit a fade to the right. If I did, it should come back.

"You're right, Lenny, your ball went to the right, but I don't think it came back. I'm pretty sure your ball hit the roof of a house or it landed in a yard," said Paul.

Under his breath, Lenny winced. "Damn! I hope not."

Another golfer snorted. "So what if it did. That's the price of living on a golf course."

With concern, Lenny responded, "I understand what you're saying, but I hate when my ball lands in someone's yard. You never know what to expect. I shouldn't worry about it, but some homeowners can be aggressive when you retrieve your ball. So, the last thing I want is to have a confrontation with a homeowner."

Paul nodded his head. "You're right. Some homeowners

have gone to the extreme. Someone told me about a guy who lives on the Cane Garden Golf Course…"

Paul looked at each man. "This homeowner sits on his lanai with a ten gauge shotgun, watching and waiting for a golfer to hit a ball in his yard. When the golfer attempts to retrieve it, the man stands up, points his gun and boom!"

Wide eyed, Lenny said, "I hope you're kidding?"

Paul kept a straight face. "Man, I'm telling you, that particular hole is not for the weak hearted. When you stand on the tee box, your knees tremble and you say a prayer asking God to let your ball go straight. Just thinking how you might be shot because your ball lands in a yard is frightening."

Pausing, Paul cleared his throat and when he tried to continue with the story, he began stuttering, followed by an outburst of a deep belly laugh. The other guys began laughing with him. Lenny did not join in on what was supposed to be funny.

Paul slapped Lenny on the back. "I'm joking, man. You need to chill out. I mean if your ball is in someone's yard, it's not like you did it on purpose."

"I know. It's just that I don't find the subject amusing.

Lenny climbed into the golf cart. Paul followed him and sat in the driver's seat. As Paul drove off, he said, "Let's see if we can find our golf balls."

CHAPTER 4

Cee Tyson finished her breakfast and picked up her binoculars and turned her attention to the tee box. While she observed the golfers, Les, her husband, had returned to the lanai.

"What are you looking at?"

"The golfers. They've stopped golfing. They're just standing around."

Since Cee did not golf, Les explained, "That's the hole that gets backed up. The golfers don't want to take a chance of a ball hitting someone. So, they have to wait until they think it's safe to hit."

"I think golf is such a waste of time. I'll never understand why someone would want to hit a ball and then chase it." Cee put the binoculars down and picked up the newspaper.

Les was not going to allow his wife to bait him into a discussion about his favorite pastime. "Is there anything interesting in the newspaper?"

"Not really. It's a different day with the same old topics of crime, politics, and death." She folded the paper and laid it on a nearby table.

"Are you ready to get our day started?"

"Not quite yet. I'm still enjoying the view and the weather."

Les muttered under his breath. "Well, that will change soon." He said nothing further as he thought about the golfers and how much they annoyed Cee. Again, he tried to get her to go inside the house. "The temperature is rising and I think we should go inside."

Irritated, Cee blurted out. "What's the point of having a beautiful golf course view if we can only enjoy it in the evening after the golf course closes?"

Les made a face and refused to answer Cee's question. He wasn't about to spoil his morning by having a heated discussion about his suggestion to live on the golf course. He was amazed at how Cee was able to remind him daily that it was his idea to sell their courtyard villa and buy this house.

If it had not been for their next door neighbor's backyard fire and the fire department's report that it had been set deliberately, Les would never have insisted on moving. He didn't want to live in a neighborhood where a suspected arsonist might be one of their neighbors since the person was never apprehended.

The more Cee tried to convince him that his fears were unwarranted, the more adamant he became. Cee agreed to move, but only if they bought a designer house. Then Les reacted by insisting that the house be on a golf course. After weeks of battling the issue back and forth similar to a tennis match, Les won.

"Is everything okay, Les?"

"Everything's fine." He stood up in hopes that Cee would follow. He wanted to get her inside the house before the golfers advanced down the fairway or worse, a badly hit ball would land in the yard.

Cee continued sitting and looking through the binoculars. As Les turned to go inside, Cee screamed, "Watch out!"

CHAPTER 5

Striking shades of orange, red and yellow illuminated the early morning sky. Each morning, Woody thought how the scenery never disappointed him whether it was watching the rising sun or the evening sunset. Sitting on the lanai, he admired the awesome wonders of nature and everything it had to offer, from the hanging moss on the oak trees to the variety of palm trees.

While not a bird watcher, Woody enjoyed the show the Herons, Egrets, and Cranes were putting on as they pranced or perhaps they were dancing up and down the fairway. The sounds from all the creatures were harmony to his ears whether it was croaking frogs, buzzing insects, or chirping birds. In a short time, the soothing rustling of the trees, chirping birds, and the view that he loved would be interrupted by sounds from noisy golf carts and golfers talking and laughing.

Woody stood up, and walked into the house to the kitchen. After pouring coffee into his favorite mug, he proceeded back outside to the lanai with the newspaper tucked under his arm. Rather than be distracted by the golfers, Woody sat with his back to the golf course. He opened the newspaper and glanced through it before settling on the sports section.

"What the hell!" Something hard hit against his head, causing him to drop the newspaper.

Woody's hand flew to the back of his head. The area was sore to the touch and wet. Lowering his hand, he saw blood.

Under his breath, he cursed again, spotting the culprit that had caused the injury. When he rose from the chair and bent over to pick up the golf ball, a white light flashed before his eyes, followed by little bright dots. A tingling sensation went from the top of his head to the back of his lower neck. A sharp pain in his left side made him wrench, followed by throbbing in his temples.

Inhaling and exhaling, Woody blew air out of his opened mouth, trying to slow his rapid heartbeat. Woody waited for the golfers, his nostrils flaring and his anger building.

CHAPTER 6

As much as Woody wanted to control his temper he knew it would be impossible. When he finished giving the golfer a tongue lashing, he or she would think twice each time before teeing off on the eighth hole of the Nancy Lopez Golf Course.

Being hit in the head reminded Woody about the Jones Screen Repair Company. He had been more than patient with them. Daily, he could kick himself for not insisting on a written, signed contract when the hurricane damaged screens had been removed from the lanai.

The company had been less than truthful when they guaranteed replacements within forty-eight hours. Two months had passed and still no new screens. To add to his irritation and frustration, he had done the ultimate no-no. He had paid the company in full before any work had started.

The wrath of his words would not be the only thing the Jones Company would endure. With the help of his lawyer wife, he would sue them. The strength of his case was easy. His injury would never have occurred if the company had kept their promise.

A pained smile covered his face. "Jones Company get ready to pay poppa." The putt-putt sound of an approaching golf cart interrupted his thoughts.

Slowly, Paul drove the golf cart, searching for his ball. Lenny spotted it. "There it is."

Paul stopped the cart and climbed out. While the other guys hit their balls, he selected a club.

Lenny watched as Paul hit. "Good shot, man." Paul's ball landed within fifty feet of the green.

"Thanks, man." Paul put his club back in his bag, climbed into the cart and drove toward the edge of the fairway. "Now let's see if we can find your ball."

Driving toward the direction to where he thought Lenny's ball might have landed, Paul eased the cart to a complete stop. They glanced from right to left.

Lenny asked, "Do you see it?"

Woody watched the approaching golf cart. When he went to stand up his legs wobbled, making it difficult. He moaned when out of nowhere a hot pain shot up the left side of his face, attacking his eye. Strange tingling currents were zooming up and down his leg.

Using his right hand, Woody leaned on the table for support and eased himself up onto his feet. The burning pain made Woody raise his right hand to cover his left eye. Using his right eye, he squinted.

Woody's chest was tight, his breathing erratic. Dropping his right hand from his eye, he held up the ball he had picked up off the floor. Waiting for the golf cart to reach the house, he cursed. The golf cart had stopped.

Paul's eyes were wide. "Oh shit! I think I see your ball." He pointed. "See over there, a man is holding it up for us to see it."

Woody focused on the men in the golf cart. He admonished himself. He should have never held up the ball. He opened his mouth, but the words seemed trapped in his throat. His tongue felt thick.

While nudging Lenny's arm, Paul chuckled. "Man. What are you going to do?"

Lenny didn't have to think twice about his response. "What do you think? I'm going to drop a ball, take a penalty, and keep golfing."

Before the golf cart sped off, he put the ball down and stuck his middle finger up in the air. He watched the cart change directions and go down the fairway.

Disgusted, he banged his right fist on the table which sent a prickly electric shock down his left side. "O—O--Ouch!"

The pain caused him to forget about the golfers. Rubbing his left arm, he eased back down into the chair.

CHAPTER 7

After the eighth hole, Lenny was no longer concentrating on golf. He couldn't shake the image of the man standing on the lanai. Something was familiar about the man, leaving Lenny with the impression that he knew him.

The round of golf ended and Paul couldn't resist teasing Lenny. "Man, can you believe how good I golfed? Or was it that you golfed so badly?" Not waiting for a response, Paul hurried on. "I'm enjoying this because it isn't often I beat you at golf and win your money."

Lenny forced a laugh. "Hey, even Tiger Woods has a bad day and today was mine. I accept defeat, but there's always the next time."

Paul asked, "Do you want to have lunch or are you in a hurry?"

"Lunch would be good. Where do you want to eat?"

Paul suggested, "Why don't we eat here?"

The outside of the Nancy Lopez Country Club had a large, expansive veranda filled with beautiful white wicker chairs, rockers, and tables. The décor was inviting and warm, making Lenny feel as if he was stepping onto someone's porch rather than entering a restaurant. Inside, pictures of Nancy Lopez adorned the white, blue, and yellow painted and wallpapered walls.

Rather than eat in the main dining room, Paul directed Lenny to the bar for quicker service. They placed their food and drink orders. When Lenny had enough of Paul's taunting, he switched the conversation from golf to football.

A man sitting across the bar from them was waving his hand. After several tries, he caught their attention. "By any chance, did you guys golf at Nancy Lopez this morning?"

"Yeah, we did, why?" asked Paul.

"Because I was told a stray golf ball hit a homeowner in the head."

"Get out of here." Paul nudged Lenny. Lenny stiffened.

Before the man could continue with the details, the bartender interrupted with a question. "How did it happen?"

The man snickered. "It's called collateral damage for living on a golf course."

The bartender shrugged. "I don't golf, so what does that mean?"

The man explained. "A homeowner has to expect just about anything when living on a golf course. A stray golf ball might hit the roof of a house, break a window or land on a beautifully landscaped lawn."

Lenny inquired with a concerned tone. "Was the homeowner's injury bad?"

CHAPTER 8

After taking several deep breaths, Woody closed and opened his eyes. Praying, he wanted the pain to stop. When it didn't, he yelled, "Man-man-dee—Man—man—dee!"

Catching his breath, he yelled again. "Man-man—man—dee. Man—man—dee!"

Confused by the awkwardness of the sounds coming out of his mouth, Woody paused. Putting his hand to this throat, he swallowed hard. Again, he called out to Mandy.

To his ears, his words sounded garbled and unintelligent. He was reminded of when he was being examined by the doctor, looking down his throat while he used a wooden depressor, asking him questions. He wondered how the doctor understood his responses.

To ease his pain, he moved his hand from his throat to the side of his face. Novocain was the only way Woody could describe how his face felt. In addition, his head was throbbing and beads of sweat had formed on his forehead and upper lip. Overall, his skin was wet and clammy.

Annoyed, Woody yelled again, "Man-man-dee, Man-man-dee." He wondered, "Why was she taking so long?"

Waiting for his wife, Woody was reminded of a television commercial. In the past, he had laughed at the woman who lies on the floor, vulnerable and pleading, "I've fallen and I can't get up." Now he could identify with the stricken woman and it wasn't funny.

Through gritted teeth, Amanda responded, "Okay, Woody. I'll be there in a minute."

Woody called her name a second and then a third time, Amanda rolled her eyes. Irritated, she exhaled noisily and began counting, one, two, three.... She yelled, "Woody, I'm coming."

Amanda thought this was just another one of Woody's ploys to make her quit her job. He started by calling her job with all types of emergencies, from cutting his finger to locking his keys in the car.

When none of the tactics worked, Woody began disrupting her mornings by creating distractions that would make her late for work. She was sure he hoped she would be fired if she wouldn't resign.

After the fifth day of trying to make her late, Amanda began ignoring his yells and demands. She knew he didn't want anything of importance. Rather than lose her temper and start her day off on the wrong foot, she made every attempt to overlook his childish behavior.

Amanda continued putting on her makeup even though Woody kept yelling. "Today, Mr. Roberts, you will have to wait until I'm finished." She blew out a loud puff of air. Pursing her lips, she said loudly through clenched teeth, "Woody, I'm coming."

CHAPTER 9

As Amanda approached the lanai, she spotted Woody slumped down in the chair. Rushing through the open sliding glass door, she bent close to Woody's face. "Woody! Woody!"

As Amanda examined him, she spotted blood on the back of his head. Grabbing the cordless phone, she dialed 911.

Guilt consumed her body as she waited for someone to answer. How could she have been so thoughtless? Why didn't she respond to his loud cries?

Amanda swiped at a falling tear, trying to keep the panic out of her voice. She told the operator to send an ambulance and why. She ended the call and turned her attention back to Woody.

"Honey, the paramedics should be here shortly. Sit still and don't move." Soothingly, she stroked his hand.

"Everything is going to be just fine." Her words sounded confident, but from all indications she could see that something was seriously wrong with Woody.

The wait was unbearable. Every time she glanced at the clock, it was as if the hands had stopped moving. Finally, she heard the blaring siren. Leaving Woody, Amanda rushed to the door, letting the paramedics in.

They followed her to the lanai and quickly, they went about doing their job. Amanda watched as they expertly took Woody's vitals, asked questions, and phoned the hospital with initial findings.

The two paramedics lifted Woody and placed him on a stretcher. Before leaving the house, the medium height, female paramedic turned to Amanda. "We're transporting Mr. Roberts to The Villages' Hospital. Are you going to ride in the ambulance with your husband?"

"No. I'll follow you in my car."

Inside the ambulance, Woody's eyes were closed. He remembered answering questions and something sharp sticking his arm. He guessed he was on his way to the hospital.

Everything seemed dream-like. Bright lights were blinding him, but he thought he saw Mandy. Why was she dressed in white, appearing like an angel? He wondered if this could be the end.

Of all things, he wondered why she was telling him how much she had hated their initial move to Florida. They had relocated from Michigan to a retirement community in Tampa and daily, Mandy expressed her dislike for it.

Her complaint was the lifestyle. She wanted more than shuffleboard, bingo, and people talking about their aches and pains, and latest medical procedures. He should have known better than to move a vibrant, thirty-eight year-old to a slow-paced environment with everyone being at least twenty to thirty years her senior.

The move to Florida and Woody's retirement had put them at odds until he discovered The Villages. At first Mandy was not sold on moving to another retirement community. After visiting The Villages and Woody giving her a sales-pitch as if he worked for them, Mandy gave in with the condition that if she didn't like it, they would move back to Michigan.

The moving vehicle stopped and the doors opened. Inside the hospital, the paramedics pushed the stretcher at a brisk pace down the corridor. The gurney ride was unstable. Woody's body was pulled, jerked, and turned, all in one motion. The movement made his head swirl which caused dizziness. He hoped the ride would soon end.

When the gurney came to a halt Woody heard a man's voice. *"On my count, ready, one, two, three."* Woody's body was lifted and placed onto a stationery bed.

Although Woody's eyes were closed, his eyelids fluttered upon hearing a man's voice. "Mr. Roberts! Can you hear me? Mr. Roberts! I'm Dr. Timmons."

CHAPTER 10

Amanda rushed through the automatic doors. Taking quick steps, she approached the blondish-gray-haired woman sitting at the information desk. She had a volunteer button pinned to the hospital issued vest.

"Excuse me. My husband, Woodward Roberts, was just brought in here. Can you tell me where he was taken?"

"Yes, your husband is here." She chirped, tilting her head towards a closed door. "He's in the back, being seen by a doctor." The voice became firm, but polite. "However, before you can see your husband, you need to complete some forms."

Amanda murmured, "thank you."

Without missing a beat, Amanda took long strides towards the closed door. As her hand reached for the door knob, the woman she had ignored shouted, "Stop!"

The authoritative words, "You can't go in there," did not prevent Amanda from opening the door. She was taken aback with the flurry of activity. People dressed in a variety of colorful matching tops and bottoms were moving about in a hurried but efficient manner.

"Excuse me." Amanda stopped a woman, she assumed to be a nurse. "Can you help me?"

"I'll try."

"I was told my husband Woodward Roberts was back here, seeing a doctor. Can you tell me where I can find him?"

"He's not one of my patients. Go to the nurse's station and someone will help you."

"Thanks."

The nurse's desk matched the surrounding activity. The telephone was ringing and a number of buttons on the console were flashing. As if programmed the young man at the station handed charts and folders to anyone requesting them without looking at them. Before he was able to acknowledge Amanda, the man answered another incoming call. After completing the phone call, he asked, "How may I help you?"

"I'm looking for Woodward Roberts."

Quickly, he scanned a piece of paper. "He's in the room to the left."

"Thank you."

Amanda's stomach was churning, not knowing what to expect. Taking a deep breath, she pulled back the drawn curtain. With eyes wide, her mouth fell open.

"Where was Woody? Maybe, she misunderstood which room he was in."

Turning around, she collided into a woman. "I'm sorry."

"No problem. May I help you?"

"I'm looking for Woodward Roberts. I was told he was in here."

"You have the right room. The doctor saw him and ordered some tests. It could take awhile before he comes back. I suggest you go back out into the waiting room."

Disappointment covered Amanda's face. "Before I go, can you tell me how he's doing?"

"You'll have to wait and talk to the doctor."

CHAPTER 11

Helplessness struck Amanda again as she walked back out into the waiting area. Unfortunately, she didn't know anymore than when she first entered into the hospital.

Guilt made her question, why she didn't accompany Woody by ambulance to the hospital instead of driving? She admonished herself. Nothing would be gained now by her second guessing everything she had done to this point.

At first Amanda thought about sneaking pass the woman at the information desk, but that would be cowardly, especially since she was wrong. The woman was only doing her job. Straightening her shoulders, she approached the woman, prepared for what she thought could be an unpleasant situation.

"I apologize for not following your instructions. I was worried about my husband. The last thing I wanted at the time was to be told to fill out some bureaucratic paperwork."

The once friendly voice was now terse. "Take a number, have a seat and someone will call your name."

This time, Amanda obeyed. Before she could settle into the seat, her name was called. The smile on Amanda's face soon changed when a different woman handed her a clipboard.

"Please fill in the highlighted areas on all the forms. When you finish, please bring everything back to me."

Taking the clipboard, Amanda sat down. Hospital procedures are annoying. Irritated, she wrote firmly on each form. All she wanted was information about Woody's condition and all the hospital wanted was to make sure he had medical insurance and the ability to pay for services rendered.

With all the forms completed, she returned them as instructed. The woman took the forms from Amanda and inspected each page. "Thank you."

Amanda remained standing. Firmly and with an attitude, the woman said, "You can take a seat. Someone should be with you shortly."

Amanda wanted to protest, but instead, she did what she was

told. To occupy the time, she picked up a magazine and flipped through it, not reading a single word. Getting bored with the page turning, she placed the magazine back in the rack.

Where was Woody? How could she ever forgive herself? Before the tears started flowing, the double wood doors opened and everyone's attention went to the man dressed in green.

"Mrs. Roberts. Mrs. Roberts." Amanda stood up and walked towards the doctor. She extended her hand. "I'm Mrs. Roberts."

"I'm Dr. Timmons."

Annoyance caused a succession of questions to fly from Amanda's mouth. "How is Woody doing? Exactly, what's wrong with him? Is he going to be okay?"

CHAPTER 12

Dr. Timmons waved his hand toward two empty chairs. "Mrs. Roberts, let's move over here." He sat down and motioned her to do the same. Amanda didn't want to sit. She wanted answers, but she did as the doctor had suggested.

"Your husband had a stroke."

Amanda whispered. "What are you saying? My husband had a head injury. I don't understand."

"When your husband came into the ER, I examined his head wound which was superficial. It didn't even require stitches. While I was examining him I became concerned with other symptoms such as his difficulty to speak and the weaknesses on the left side of his body."

"Did the head injury cause the stroke?"

"Strokes are mysteries because there isn't just one specific thing that might have caused the stroke. There may have been many contributing factors such as high blood pressure, high cholesterol, or other medical reasons. It's hard to identify the exact cause."

Confused and irritated, Amanda threw her hands in the air. "Then, how do you know Woody had a stroke?"

Dr. Timmons voice was calm. "To confirm my suspicions, I ordered a MRI which can usually detect a stroke within minutes of its onset. The results indicated that your husband had a stroke."

Watching Mrs. Roberts about to pounce on his last statement, he rushed on. "Without being too technical, there are two types of strokes. One type is caused by blood clots or other matter. The other type is caused by the bleeding from a burst blood vessel."

"Do you know which one Woody had?"

"Before I make the final diagnosis, I'm running a series of tests. After the results, I'll be able to determine which type he had."

Tears cascaded down Amanda's face. She sniffed and

cleared her throat. "What type of tests?"

"Right now, he's having a CT Scan which is just a series of pictures of his brain to determine whether there is any bleeding."

Amanda tugged at her lip. "Will that be it?"

"No, I've ordered an EKG to check his heart and a number of blood tests. All the tests will help in making choices about the treatment for his recovery."

Amanda shrugged and looked at the doctor as if he had been speaking a foreign language.

Dr. Timmons watched Mrs. Roberts pull at her manicured, red colored fingernails. Her head was bent as if she was processing everything he had told her.

"I know I've thrown a lot of information at you, but let's wait until the tests are complete and then I can be more exact with the information about his condition."

Dr. Timmons stood up, indicating he was finished. As he walked away, Amanda ran after him.

"Dr. Timmons. Dr. Timmons, wait." He turned around.

"When can I see my husband?"

"You can see him after the tests are completed."

CHAPTER 13

After seeing the golf ball hit their neighbor, Cee was troubled about the accident. "What else can happen? I told you Les that owning a house on a golf course was dangerous."

Pacing back and forth, Cee went on and on about the golfers. Most of all she wanted to do something to retaliate against the golfers involved in the recent offenses. "We need to do something or at least tell someone about this."

Les wished there was something he could say or do to calm Cee down. As far as he was concerned there was very little they could do. However, he wasn't about to tell Cee that.

Soothingly, Les asked, "What would you like to do?"

"Well, I don't know, but…" Cee picked up the phone and was placing a call.

The week was turning more bizarre with each telephone call. Again, Dan was stunned. He laughed. Could something be in the drinking water? What was going on in The Villages?

All of a sudden, homeowners living on the golf course are having problems with golfers. To make matters worse, they want the police to take some sort of action.

The most recent phone call was from a woman who insisted on filing a formal complaint against a golfer. According to the woman, the man, her neighbor, was standing on his lanai when a golf ball hit him in the head. To make matters worse, the woman couldn't provide any specific details regarding the golfer, like a name or a description of the man. The bottom line was that there was nothing the police could do about the incident.

Les had no idea who Cee had called until she began talking.

From her expression, Les knew the police's response wasn't what she had expected.

After she put the phone in the cradle, Les asked, "What did the police say?"

"They thanked me and said there was nothing they could do. In addition, they told me that the next time something like this happened, I should obtain the golfer's name."

Cee stopped. "This is exactly why people take matters into their own hands."

"Honey Bun, the police are merely doing their job."

"Don't you dare agree with the police!"

"I'm not. It's just that…"

"I'll tell you what, since I couldn't identify the man who did the crime, let's use our energy to find out who our injured neighbor is."

CHAPTER 14

With Les' index finger, he touched his lip. "That's a good idea, but how do we go about finding out who he is?"

"I can use my cookies." Cee's eyes twinkled. "They always get results." She clapped her hands. "I have an idea. We'll drive to the street where we think he lives and knock on doors, pretending to be new in The Villages. Our entrance into each home will be my cookies and then I'll ask my questions."

With pride, Les puffed out his chest and grinned. The police could learn a thing or two from Cee regarding how to interrogate people. Over the years, she had used her homemade cookies and the *'I'm just a little old lady routine'* to obtain all types of information and no one ever suspected what she was doing.

"Les, we need to hurry. That man could be dead."

Smothering a laugh, Les patted her hand. "The man isn't dead. Remember, we saw the paramedics put him on a stretcher." Les paused. "Wait a minute. I bet the man was taken to The Villages'…."

Cee butted in. "You're right, Les. Why didn't I think of that?"

Mumbling, she stood up. "I hope I'm not losing my investigative skills."

"I don't think you have to worry about that. The accident was traumatic for you."

Smiling she stood up before going to the kitchen. "We might get lucky. Remember, I used to volunteer at the hospital and maybe one of my friends will be working today. If that's the case, getting the information will be as easy as it is for me to bake my cookies. Now, let's get ready to go."

After Les and Cee showered and dressed, they drove to the hospital. Upon entering the hospital doors, Cee's eyes widened. Nudging Les, she whispered, "Look who is working."

They hurried over to the information desk. Cheerfully, Cee chirped, "Good morning, Shirley."

Jumping up, Shirley greeted Cee with a friendly hug. Releasing Cee from her embrace, Shirley exclaimed. "What a surprise! How are you? What brings you to the hospital?"

CHAPTER 15

Holding up the basket of cookies, Cee smiled. "I haven't seen any of the volunteers in a long time. I thought you all might like some of my homemade cookies."

"How thoughtful and everyone loves your cookies."

Les watched Cee work her magic.

"Shirley, the one thing I admire about you is that you always seem to know what's going on at the hospital, not just with the hospital staff, but even people being admitted." Shirley bobbed her head in agreement.

"I was wondering if you've been here all morning."

"Yes. Why?"

Cee leaned close to Shirley. "Well, I need your help." Glancing around, Cee made sure no one could hear her. "A man, actually he's our neighbor. He was hit in the head by a stray golf ball."

Wide-eyed, Shirley said, "Really! How did it happen?"

"Well, I was sitting on our lanai. A golfer hit his ball. Instead of it landing in the fairway it veered off and it struck the man in the head."

Shirley shook her head, not a single heavily sprayed gray hair moved. "I tell people all the time that I wouldn't own a house on a golf course if they gave it to me. It's too dangerous."

Stopping, she titled her head to the side. "Wait a minute. Did you say you witnessed this while sitting on your lanai…but you don't live…wait, did you move?

Cee inhaled and exhaled before answering. "It's a long story, but yes, we moved. We bought a house on the Nancy Lopez Golf Course. Why don't we have lunch and I'll tell you all about it."

Shirley's face turned red, but she didn't apologize for her earlier statement. "I would love to do lunch."

"Great. By any chance was a man admitted to the hospital with a head injury?"

"Let me see." Shirley flipped through the newly admitted

patients' list and looked at Cee before she continued the search. "You know I won't have information about why a person was admitted but...." She paused.

"Uh...let's see. There were only two recently admitted patients, a woman and a man. Mr. Woodward Roberts is probably the man you're looking for."

Now that Cee obtained the information she wanted, she was ready to leave. Cee didn't have time to listen to Shirley's idle chitchat and gossip about people she no longer knew.

"Girl, I really appreciate your help, but we have a number of errands to run. Do you know if Mr. Roberts can receive visitors?"

"Yes. He's in Room 341A."

"Girl, you're a doll. Keep up the good work. What would I do without friends like you?"

As Les and Cee walked toward the elevator, Cee turned around. "Thanks again. I'll call you soon for lunch."

CHAPTER 16

The elevator ride was quiet except for the mechanical humming as it went up. When the elevator stopped, they exited and walked down the corridor. Cee didn't need any help finding Mr. Roberts room since she had volunteered on this floor.

Rather than wait for someone to respond to Les' light rap on the door, he and Cee walked in. Their entrance brought awkwardness with them.

Cee scanned the room. Only one bed was occupied so she assumed the man in the bed was Mr. Roberts. The man was distinguished looking and may have been in his late sixties or early seventies. The bed did not hide the man's imposing stature.

Sitting in a chair, was an attractive woman with striking features. A mature Janet Jackson, the singer, came to Cee's mind.

The woman broke the silence. Her voice was soft and pleasant. "Hello. May I help you?"

"I'm sorry. My name is Cee Cee Tyson, but everyone calls me Cee." She made a gesture. "And, this is my husband Les. We're your neighbors. Well, kind of. We live directly across the golf course from your house."

Les cleared his throat. "We're looking for Mr. Roberts."

Before Woody answered the man, he thought the couple resembled two famous personalities. The man resembled Mr. Rogers who was on television, tall, thin, and neighborly. The wife was a shoe-in for Mrs. Santa Claus with her stout figure, gray hair, and wire rimmed glasses sitting on the end of her nose. The only thing missing was an apron.

"I'm…I'm Wood…Woodward Ro…Ro…Roberts."

Although Mr. Roberts stuttered, Cee thought his deep baritone voice made him sound authoritative as well as threatening.

Woody tried not to laugh as he listened to Mrs. Santa Claus. "We promise not to take up too much of your time. We care about our neighbors' welfare and that's why we're here. First of all, we're sorry you had to experience such an awful injury."

Cee glanced at the Roberts, making sure they were paying attention. "We felt compelled to come to the hospital. We thought it was our duty and the right thing to do."

Woody and Amanda exchanged glances as Mr. Tyson started talking. "I'll get right to the point. This morning while my wife was sitting on the lanai she watched the golfer hit his ball that caused your head injury."

Cee started talking over Les. "Mr. Roberts, I don't know about you and your wife, but we find the golfers to be rude and inconsiderate especially when they retrieve their mishit balls that land in the yard. We need a plan to combat their behavior."

The only response from Mr. and Mrs. Roberts was raised eye brows and pursed lips. Cee dismissed their expressions.

"I was appalled when I saw the ball strike your head. Is there anything we can do to help?"

"D…did you g…g…get the golfer's name?"

"Well, no but I made a formal complaint with the police and…."

That caught Woody's attention. "Wh….wh…what did they say?"

"They said there was nothing they could do because…."

Woody's tone turned harsh. "Then what can y…y…you do for me?"

Amanda placed her hand on Woody's thigh. He glared at her. Mrs. Roberts' voice was friendly. "We're glad to see our neighbors are concerned, but as my husband said, without knowing the golfer's name, there isn't much that can be done."

Les said, "We're sorry we can't be more of a help, but…." He touched Cee's arm.

Cee smiled. "Oh my. I almost forgot. I brought you a basket of homemade cookies. I'm told my cookies have a way of helping whatever ails you, similar to chicken soup." She laughed. "That is unless you're watching your weight or you're Diabetic."

Again, the Roberts said nothing. Cee pushed the basket toward Mrs. Roberts who reluctantly took it.

"Thank you. That was thoughtful of you."

Les pulled out his wallet and handed Amanda a card that had their name, address, and telephone number on it.

Amanda glanced at it. "Again, thank you for coming." As if an afterthought, she added, "And, thanks for the cookies."

Outside of Mr. Roberts' room, Cee leaned close to Les and whispered. "The Roberts didn't seem to appreciate our visit."

Les put his arm around Cee. "It's okay. We did the right thing."

CHAPTER 17

The hospital stay left Woody's body weaker than he had imagined. After being released from the hospital he was transferred to the Regal Care Assisted Living Facility, near The Villages.

At first Woody did not want to leave the hospital, but once he arrived at Regal Care he changed his mind. The name, *"regal,"* was truly fitting. The outside was mansion-like with tall white pillars and a circular brick driveway.

The inside appeared formal with its hardwood floors covered with oriental rugs with a blend of antique and modern furnishings. However, the atmosphere was similar to being in someone's home. The staff was responsive, caring, and friendly.

The rooms were spacious and each patient could decorate as they pleased. Since Woody did not plan on staying long, the only personal items he had Mandy bring were his two favorite five by seven framed pictures of the two of them.

The physical and speech therapy was intense, demanding, and exhausting. Woody worked hard at doing all the exercises. His willpower, diligence, and commitment paid off. In less than a month he was released to go home.

Before leaving Regal Care, Woody was given written and oral instructions. The physical therapist's instructions sounded more like orders. "Once a day, you will walk thirty minutes a day and lift the free weights three times a week." He handed Woody a piece of paper with the written exercises outlined."

The speech therapist stated, "Before you leave, I've make arrangements for an outpatient speech therapist to visit once a week."

Dr. Timmons was firm and explicit. "I want to re-emphasize what the physical therapists said about the importance of exercising. As a reminder, your physical activities are limited, meaning you should not golf, bowl, or play tennis." The doctor hesitated and rushed on. "That also means no sex."

###

Since his accident, he no longer had to worry about golf balls hitting him in the head. With a threat of a lawsuit, Jones not only apologized for the delay, but they enclosed the lanai in acrylic at no cost.

Woody's limited activities caused him to spend most of his time sitting on the lanai, reading, meditating, and watching television and the golfers. Every day the sight of the golfers reminded him of his injury.

One morning while sitting on the lanai, a golf ball landed in the yard. When the golfer sprang from the stopped golf cart, he appeared friendly. "Good morning. Nice morning for golfing."

Woody's response was a slight nod of the head. He watched and waited for the golfer to ask if he could retrieve his ball. Instead, the golfer acted as if he had never spoken to Woody.

The man stepped into the yard, took his golf club and pulled the ball from underneath the rose bush. Rather than place the ball back onto the fairway, the man hit the ball from the yard.

Woody was appalled by the action, but he said nothing. He closed his eyes and counted to ten. The only reason he was able to control his emotions was because he didn't want his progress impeded in any way.

Maybe Woody spent too much time on the lanai, but he kept track of the number of times a golf ball landed in the yard. With each incident, the golfers seemed to be more arrogant, rude, and inconsiderate. Now, he understood what Cee Tyson had said. Something had to be done to combat the golfers.

Determined to tackle the golfers' behavior, Woody began to devise a plan. Developing it had given Woody renewed energy and motivation to work hard on his rehab. Twice a day, he took a thirty minute walk. Three times a week, he lifted free weights, and every day he did his reading and speaking exercises. He knew progress had been made when the speech therapist announced that Woody no longer needed to see him on a weekly basis.

Mandy was impressed and encouraging. "Woody, you're doing great. At this rate, you'll be back to your old self again. Keep up the good work."

If she only knew what was driving him so hard to get well. She would not be happy. What Mandy couldn't understand was that everyone coped differently when it came to life changes.

Woody never shared with Mandy the effect of losing his first wife to cancer had on his life. For three years he watched her fight a losing battle. If he had to do it again, he would have placed her in a nursing home. Watching her suffer was too much. After her death, he had the support of relatives, friends, and a grief support group, but all of that did not stop him from becoming depressed, bitter, and angry.

Being alone was not easy. Everything he did reminded him of his loss—attending parties and family outings, taking trips, going to the movies, dining at restaurants and most of all going to bed at night.

His saving grace was Mandy. He met her when he was at the brink of deciding whether he wanted to live or die. Just when he thought he had found happiness and had begun adjusting to his later years of life, he was now experiencing another life change—the injury and stroke.

Despite what the doctor said, he believed that had it not been for the golfer, he would never have had the stroke. Although he couldn't change the fact of suffering from a stroke, he believed he could even the playing field between him and the golfers.

CHAPTER 18

Since Cee and Les had visited Mr. Roberts in the hospital, all Cee could talk about was how stray balls landing in the yard was nothing in comparison to being injured. The only solution was for them to move, Cee suggested one morning.

"Cee, you know that's not possible. With the housing market no longer lucrative we cannot move." Les made every effort to reassure her that they were safe. "Honey Cakes, do you trust me?"

She nodded her head.

"As an avid golfer, I guarantee that what happened to Mr. Roberts was a fluke."

Les paused and rubbed his chin. "I've golfed for over thirty years." He looked upward. "I've only witnessed one person who had been struck by a golf ball. A golfer teed off too soon and the ball hit another golfer who was in the fairway."

"Well that might be, but I want to take some kind of precaution that what happened to Mr. Roberts won't happen to us."

"Besides move, what do you want to do?"

Cee had no suggestions, but daily she talked about protecting their property as well as their safety.

Usually, Les listened and let her rant, offering no solutions. While reading the morning newspaper, he spotted an advertisement that might end Cee's fears. He lowered the paper and handed the ad to Cee.

"We could have the lanai enclosed, turning it into a sunroom. We would not only gain additional living space, but add value to the house."

Cee shook her head as she countered. "Will that stop a golf ball from breaking one of the glass windows?" She added with disgust. "I agree we gain a room, but we also increase our property tax since the lanai would now be a room."

Les made another suggestion. His eyes twinkled as he thought he had come up with the ultimate answer. "What about having the lanai enclosed with acrylic? It's similar to glass and there would be no tax increase."

Les hurried on before Cee objected. "In addition, there would be no glass to break. Instead, the ball will bounce off the acrylic."

"Absolutely not!" Cee was adamant. "I don't want people thinking we can't afford the glass enclosure and settled for acrylic."

Frustrated, Les ran his hand through his hair. As much as he wanted to argue the point he knew no matter how sound his suggestion was Cee had made up her mind. Les was at his wits end and didn't know how to resolve the golf course issues. His biggest fear was that Cee would take matters into her own hands.

CHAPTER 19

From the lanai, using binoculars, a homeowner observed the golf course workers. Each day, the homeowner made notes, writing down information about the workers' routine and anything else that may have been pertinent to help the owner.

While the homeowner waited for the worker to appear thoughts about living on the golf course emerged. Golf was supposed to be a genteel sport, not one with arrogant, rude individuals who didn't care about anything except for their round of golf. The homeowner knew that this was not the attitude of all golfers. Unfortunately, everyone would be sent a message since it was likely that the offenders would never believe they were the ones doing anything wrong.

The homeowner had learned that the Nancy Lopez Golf Course maintenance duties were divided into different work areas. Only one worker, a man, the same man, was assigned to the area the homeowner was most interested in monitoring.

The worker was an integral part of implementing the plan. The most difficult part of the plan was to be able to communicate with the worker. As difficult as it would be, the homeowner would find a way.

###

In the dark of the morning before the golf course is filled with golfers, the golf course crew arrives, going about their duties before the first tee time of the day.

Most golfers could care less about what happens before their scheduled tee time. They just know they want the course mowed and the greens prepared before teeing off. In addition, the golfers want workers gone and their duties finished so as not to hinder their round of golf in any way.

As the worker was about to climb onto the mower, he spotted an envelope taped to the seat. Curiously, he stared at it, wondering if it was meant for him. After he finished his shift he would see what was in the envelope.

The homeowner was anxious, excited, and curious. "Did the worker find the message?"

CHAPTER 20

Les and Cee decided to change their morning routine and eat their breakfast on the lanai. Cee was convinced that this was just one way of protecting their property. Les disagreed, but after forty-five years of being married to Cee, he knew it was better to go along to get along.

Daily, Cee expressed her desire to live in a quiet, safe environment. She could not help but think about why they had moved. Les wanted safety. Since their move, she wondered if her nosiness had cost them their peace-of-mind, friends, nice neighbors, and now their safety.

With breakfast over, Cee was about to take the last of the dishes inside when a golf ball landed in the yard. She put the dishes down and went out into the yard.

Quickly, Cee kicked the ball to the side of the house before the approaching golf cart reached the yard. She went back onto the lanai and waited.

Cee chirped, "Good morning."

All in one motion, the golfer stopped the cart, climbed out of it and returned the greeting, "Good morning ma'am." Without missing a beat, the man strolled toward the lanai, raised his golf club and whacked at one of the bushes.

"Excuse me, but what are you doing?" Cee's voice was stern.

The golfer glanced up at Cee. "I'm looking for my golf ball. I'm shaking the bush to see if it will fall out."

Mumbling under his breath the golfer continued to strike the bush. "I know my ball landed in your yard. I thought it was somewhere in this area."

In a firm, but polite tone, Cee said, "Sir, please do not hit...." Sarcastically, she rephrased, "Excuse me. I mean, shake, the bush."

Ignoring Cee, the man continued to search for his ball. "Are you sure you didn't see my ball land in your yard?"

Through gritted teeth Cee replied. "What makes you think I

52

saw the ball land in my yard?"

The golfer's facial expression was one of disbelief. "Ma'am, I'm sure it landed in your yard." His voice was firm. "Why don't you tell me where it is and I'll be on my way."

With hands on her hips, Cee matched the man's tone. "I didn't see your ball. Why don't you move along before you destroy my bush?"

Les had joined Cee on the lanai. "What's going on?"

"Nothing! All I wanted to do was to retrieve my ball from your yard, but...."

The man who had been in the golf cart pulled on the golfer's arm. "Come on, man, let's go. It's not that important. Drop a ball, hit, and take a penalty."

Les and Cee exchanged stares at the golfer who glared at them. To Cee, his snarling grimace was threatening.

As the golfers turned around and walked away, Cee shouted, "What did you call me?"

Neither golfer responded as the golfer who had been searching for his ball, placed another ball down and hit it. Before he climbed into the golf cart, Cee opened her mouth and was about to say something when Les placed his hand on her shoulder. She peeped up at him.

"Leave it alone. They're leaving."

"Now do you understand why we need to do something? The golf course has become a war zone and we need to defend our property and ourselves. It's just a matter of how we do it!"

Every stray ball landing in the yard that crushed a flower or bush prompted Cee and Les to make a formal police report. They took a bucket of golf balls to the police station, along with pictures of golfers traipsing in their yard as well as other people's yards.

The police officer's reply was always the same. "This is not a crime. We consider this a neighborhood issue."

With each filed complaint, the police continued to suggest

they take the golfers to small claims court for broken windows and damaged landscaping or they could obtain a mediator to resolve the issues.

With the police dismissing their complaints, Cee began to think how there was strength in numbers. One morning when they were eating breakfast, Cee made a suggestion.

"Let's call an emergency meeting with our neighbors."

CHAPTER 21

Cee made up flyers and they handed them out to their neighbors. The day of the meeting, Cee was ecstatic. According to the sign-in sheet, only 10 neighbors had not attended.

Not to start the meeting off on the wrong foot, Cee began on time. She stepped up to the podium, lowering the microphone.

"Excuse me, may I have your attention." Cee raised her voice and repeated, "Excuse me, may I have your attention."

The room became quiet. "For those that don't know me, my name is Cee Cee Tyson, better known as Cee." She pointed. "And, this is my husband, Les. We have lived in The Villages for over...."

A burly man stood up. "I don't want to be rude, but can we suspend with all the personal background information and get on with the meeting." The man glanced at his watch. "I have another appointment."

Cee hoped her face did not match the anger that his comment had evoked. His tone was similar to the types of golfers she encountered from time-to-time. Before answering him, she forced a smile.

She used the most syrupy voice she could muster up. "Yes sir. This meeting was called because of golfers' inconsiderate behavior and their disregard for our property. We have to do something to stop them."

Laughter and chatter erupted. Cee raised her voice, trying to regain control of the meeting.

"Please, this is a serious matter. My husband and I have had to endure rude comments, broken windows, and trampled landscaping"

Clearing her throat, she rushed on. "In fact, did you know that a neighbor was struck in the head by a stray golf ball? His injury landed him in the hospital."

The injured homeowner, Woody had eased into the meeting after it had started. He was wearing a baseball hat and hoped that the Tysons would not recognize him.

A thin man stood up. "I'm a golfer and I'm guilty of hitting stray balls. I'm sorry about the man who was injured, but when you live on the golf course there is a certain level of risk." He paused. "I hate to say it, but that's the price of having a house on a golf course. You might want to think about moving."

A woman agreed, "My house isn't on the golf course, but I am a golfer. No golfer intends to hit a ball in anyone's yard and we certainly don't want to hit anyone. As far as our behavior, golfers do need to be more considerate. However, I'm not sure what can be done about that."

Cee ignored the man's comments and directed her response to the woman. "I live on the golf course and I think as homeowners we have rights and we just need to think of ways to combat these abuses."

Woody wanted to agree with Mrs. Tyson, but he kept quiet. For what he was planning, this meeting was certainly helping his cause. Besides, it was nice to hear that someone other than himself was ready to take some sort of action regarding the golfers.

A man up front yelled, "Have you gone to the police?"

"Uh…we have." Cee wished this question had not been asked. She cleared her throat.

"The police were less than sympathetic. They suggested that people living on the golf course resolve any disputes on our own, hire a mediator, or take these individuals to small claims court for reimbursement for any tangible damages."

Cee's response caused most of the people to make similar comments. *"Well, if the police aren't going to help then there isn't much that can be done. This meeting is a waste of time and energy. Besides, we do live in a golf course community."*

Woody slipped out of the meeting before it ended. He was sure no one came up with a solution, but perhaps one person other than him was willing to do something about the problem.

Before the meeting ended, Cee and Les thanked them for listening and told everyone to have some cookies and punch. While people enjoyed the refreshments, Cee and Les talked to the neighbors, individually, but again no one wanted to brainstorm ideas to combat the problem.

Some neighbors didn't want to deal with the problem at all. Others stated they had not experienced any type of skirmish that had been mentioned.

The consensus was to follow the police suggestions and that each homeowner should deal with the golfers on their own.

CHAPTER 22

With the fading sun, a slight breeze could be felt in the air. Soon it would be dusk and then nightfall. Waiting for the darkness to cover the sky, Woody changed his clothes and made final preparations.

Patience was needed if he was going to pull off the plan successfully. He made himself a glass of iced tea and sat on the lanai.

For once he was happy Mandy had a job. Most of all, her occasional late work schedule provided him with the opportunity to do what he was about to do without suspicion.

Sipping the tea, Woody thought about his incredible luck. He didn't even have to worry about his neighbors. On the left, the couple was seasonal residents. He hated that term. They were snowbirds! Just like birds, they stayed up north until bad weather was predicted. Then, they flocked to the warmer climate, just like birds, seeking temporary residency.

The Witherspoons lived on the right and they were on a cruise. If he remembered correctly, this was cruise number thirty-four and they would be gone for twenty-eight days. Woody couldn't understand why anyone would take that many cruises.

After the first and only cruise he had taken, he swore nothing could lure him back on that so called, *"floating hotel,"* even if all expenses were paid. He thought about the cabins that were nothing more than big walk-in closets, equipped with beds. The eye-appealing cuisine was in abundance and available 24/7, but most of it was flavorless, no different than bland hospital food.

The nightly entertainment, featuring singing and dancing was amateurish. For those seeking other night-time entertainment, gambling was available. The biggest draw was the slot machines and from the loud ringing and flashing lights, one would think there were lots of winners. The reality was there was only an occasional *"big"* winner.

The last annoying part of cruising was the passengers who

were a tad too friendly. They struck up conversations as if they were your long-lost friend or relative. The only positive attributes, as he saw it, was room service and the nightly chocolates left on the pillow.

On the other side of the Witherspoons lived the Dillards. They were probably off visiting their darling grandchildren or maybe it was for some other reason. It didn't matter, what was important was that they were away for a month.

At last, the darkness blanketed the sky. Woody had dressed in black jeans, black T-Shirt, and a black hooded jacket. Originally, he was going to wear a black ski mask, but with the latest rash of house break-ins, he quickly dismissed that idea, fearful he would be mistaken for a burglar. Pulling the jacket hood over his head would be enough to conceal his identity. He picked up the black back-pack like bag and slung it over his shoulder.

Walking out the lanai door, Woody blew out quick breaths of air, trying to calm his nerves. He walked to the edge of the golf course fairway and then crouched down low to the ground. Awkwardly, Woody moved at a snail's pace. Letting out a slight chuckle, he thought about the children's game, duck, duck, goose.

Since it was dark, the neighbors situated across the golf course should have difficulty seeing him. If spotted, he hoped they might not know if he were human or animal. The image of being mistaken for a big black bear made Woody laugh until he thought about the possibility of being shot.

CHAPTER 23

The meeting did not discourage Les and Cee. They forged ahead and became vigilant about gathering evidence against trespassing golfers. In addition to filing police complaints, they began making reports to the golf course Starters and to the Ambassadors, as appropriate. They also continued taking pictures.

After lunch, Les and Cee were watching the afternoon news when suddenly Cee jumped up. She started pulling drawers out, rummaging through papers and business cards.

"What are you looking for?"

Rather than answer Les, she shouted, "I found it." She held up a business card. "I'm going to call the developer, Mr. Kindle."

"What? Why? What do you have in mind?"

"I think he'll want to know what's going on in his development. Let's face it The Villages is no different than any other business. He can't afford bad publicity."

Les would have liked to have used the number differently. He wasn't sure it was wise to use it for this. He wanted to discuss it, but it was too late, Cee was already dialing the number.

"Hello. May I please speak to Mr. Kindle?"

"Yes, may I ask who is calling?"

"My name is Mrs. Cee Cee Tyson. I met Mr. Kindle at a Republican Party fundraiser. He told me that if I ever needed anything to call him."

"May I ask the nature of the call?"

Cee hedged. Quickly, she thought about the phrase she had heard on many television programs and it always seemed to work. "It's personal."

"Please hold."

Cee Cee wasn't sure if Mr. Kindle would remember her, let alone take her call.

After hearing who was on the line Mr. Kindle didn't want to

take the call, but thought he had no choice. Mr. and Mrs. Tyson had been generous when giving to the Republican Party. He didn't want to lose that type of a benefactor.

Before she could tell Les what she was thinking a male's voice came on the line.

"Hello, Mrs. Tyson. How have you been?"

"I'm fine. I wasn't sure you would remember me, let alone take my call. I appreciate it and since I know you're a busy man I'll get right to the point. I live on the Nancy Lopez Golf Course and as a homeowner, I'm having a problem."

"What type of problem?"

Cee hesitated, she should have given this more thought as she considered how to proceed. "My husband is a golfer and we understand that those living on the golf course will experience some level of broken windows, balls landing on the roof, and damage to the landscape."

Mr. Kindle interrupted Cee, his voice sounding unsympathetic. "Before you continue, I have no intention of …." He admonished himself. Rather than appear as if he was dismissing her, he asked, "What do you want me to do?"

Cee was surprised. "Well…uh…." She was seldom lost for words, but quickly responded. "Maybe an article could appear in the newspaper that discusses the importance of golfers being courteous to homeowners or maybe you could convince the police to at least look into our complaints."

A long silence invaded the phone before Mr. Kindle responded. "Let me think about it."

Before Cee could say another word, he hung up, thanking her for calling.

CHAPTER 24

Watching Cee take off her glasses and close her eyes, Les knew she didn't get the response she had hoped for when placing the call to Mr. Kindle.

"Cee, are you okay?"

"At least he didn't blow me off. He said he would think about my suggestions."

"That's something."

"Yeah, but it isn't enough. I wanted him to at least say he would get back to me. To be honest, he was polite, but I don't think he wanted to hear about it." Cee sniffed. "Les, what are we going to do?"

"It's okay Sugar Bunny." Les hugged her. "You're my hero and you're doing everything you possibly can to fight this battle."

Cee pulled away from Les. "We're in this by ourselves and we'll have to attack this like a couple of pit bulls."

He was firm. "Cee, we must agree that we aren't going to confront the golfers."

"What do you mean?"

"You know what I mean. We need to remain calm and not provoke anyone into an argument."

Les warned. "We don't want to put ourselves in any kind of danger." He was concerned because over the past months Cee's behavior had become aggressive when approaching golfers who attempted to retrieve a golf ball from the yard.

"One thing for sure, the concealed weapons law is on our side." She laughed. "Before shooting a golfer, I wonder what I would have to do to show how threatened I felt."

Wide eyed and opened mouthed Les could not believe what his wife was saying. The gun and permit they had obtained was not something that should be taken lightly. The gun was for their protection if someone entered their home and for no other reason.

Cee watched the shocked look on Les' face and started

laughing. "I was joking. I wouldn't shoot anyone. I'll be on my best behavior when talking to golfers who trespass on our property. Better yet, I'll make every attempt to keep my mouth shut."

Cee hurried on. "I assure you, I'm not going to shoot anyone, but I am going to explore other ways to deal with these golfers."

CHAPTER 25

The golf club robberies and now homeowners arguing with golfers, what else is going to happen? Mr. Kindle picked up the phone and dialed Dan Wong's number.

"Hello Mr. Kindle. What's up?"

"Do you know a Mrs. Tyson?"

Of course Dan knew who Mrs. Tyson was, but why was Mr. Kindle asking if he knew her. While Dan thought about how to answer him, Mr. Kindle continued.

"She called me about golfers on the golf course. I was hoping you could shed some light on this matter. If she called me I figured she had also called the Sheriff's department."

"Yes, I know the woman." What Dan really wanted to say was that the woman was a nuisance and a nutcase. She called daily filing a report about every golfer that looked her way.

Calmly, Dan continued. "Mrs. Tyson has called and has made numerous formal complaints regarding golfers breaking her windows and destroying her landscaping."

Dan heard Mr. Kindle exhale noisily. "What have you done about this?"

"Thank God they were not having this conversation face-to-face," Dan didn't have a poker face and knew his face would have revealed his true feelings about the entire ordeal.

Carefully, he chose his words. "Actually, this isn't a crime. Each time she called, a formal report was taken. In addition, a number of suggestions were made that could help resolve some of her issues."

"That's not good enough. Make this go away."

Chewing on his lower lip, Dan made every effort to say nothing.

Before Mr. Kindle ended their conversation, he said, "Since you haven't called, I assume the golf club thieves are still out there."

CHAPTER 26

Les and Cee were sitting on the lanai, enjoying the sunset. Several weeks had passed and Les was happy that not a single golf ball had landed in their yard. Cee on the other was disappointed.

"I can't believe that not one stray ball has landed in our yard in days."

"You're right, but unlike you, I'm glad we haven't had to confront any golfers. Fortunately or unfortunately, our neighbors are the ones experiencing the broken windows, holes in the lanai screens, and trampled flowers and bushes."

Cee snorted. "It serves them right. We tried to warn them about living on a battle field and that we needed to take measures to fight the enemy."

"I know, but I hate that anyone has to…." Les' voice trailed off.

"Come on Sugar. The golfers need to understand that when they walk onto private property there are consequences.'"

Les was concerned. "Exactly what would be the consequences?"

"Nothing, I was just saying…." Cee paused. *"There was no sense in explaining revenge to Les."*

However, Cee remembered a time when Les would not have backed down from a fight. He would have welcomed a challenge, daring a golfer to take him on. She guessed that growing older had a way of changing everything. Now, Les was more passive aggressive than aggressive.

"I'm saying that for whatever reason, the golfers have developed a second sense about hitting a ball in our yard."

Les laughed. "I wish it was that simple. Trust me, when I say that most golfers can't control every ball they hit. Golfers wished they could be consistent in hitting the ball straight, every time. Even Tiger Woods has problems from time-to-time, keeping his ball in the fairway."

Cee shrugged.

Standing up, Les announced. "I'm going inside. It's almost time for the history channel special. Are you going to watch it?"

"It doesn't come on for another thirty minutes. What's the rush?"

"I want to change into my PJ's, get a cookie and a dish of Jell-O."

"Go ahead. I'll join you in a few minutes."

Cee shook her head in annoyance. Les might be her husband, but he was just like most of the neighbors. Everyone wants a solution to a problem, but when it comes to the hard work of solving it, no one wants to get their hands dirty. Stray golf balls may not be a crime, but Cee was determined to solve this problem just like she did when they lived in the villa.

After a rash of unsolved robberies occurred in their villa community, the residents formed a neighborhood watch. They patrolled the streets nightly, trying to catch whoever was responsible for the crimes. The watch was a definite deterrent because the robberies stopped. Unfortunately, the neighbors ended the watch activities even though the criminals had not been apprehended.

Unlike everyone else, Cee continued the neighborhood watch activities. She wrote down the license plates of unfamiliar cars driving or parking in the visitors' parking area and jotted down detailed descriptions of people she had never seen in the neighborhood. Once Cee identified the men she thought were robbing the construction sites and breaking into homes, she set a trap for the men that led to their capture.

Picking up the binoculars, she put them up to her eyes. Adjusting the lens, Cee looked to the left and to the right over the golf course. Something caught her eye, causing her to sit up straight and focus.

CHAPTER 27

The degree of darkness had not been factored into Woody's plan. Until he stepped out the lanai door, it never occurred to him that there would not be sufficient lighting. Carefully, he had designed what he thought was a fool-proof plan until now. The lack of light was an obstacle that could jeopardize his entire operation.

Based on Woody's calculations, the street and motion lights, and lighting from inside houses should have provided enough illumination for him to see. How wrong he had been.

Glancing around, Woody saw nothing but shadows and blackness. Now he knew what a blind person must feel when encountering new surroundings. A flashlight was in his bag, but to use it would possibly draw attention to him.

Frustration and the lack of light caused Woody to question whether he should continue. He was confused and had no idea where he was on the golf course. Most of all, his courage was floundering.

A decision had to be made soon. His lack of movement would likely increase the chances of getting caught. He was about to turn around and leave when his inner voice shouted, *"Remember what happened to you!"*

Woody took a deep breath and admonished himself. He couldn't allow a little darkness to frighten him. For weeks he had planned this and nothing would prevent him from completing his mission.

Yesterday's rain made pushing the nails into the ground easy. Woody wished he had tested his plan. He had no idea how far to shove the nails into the ground, but they had to sit up far enough to cause damage.

"Ouch," he yelled when he pushed a nail into the ground.

He took off his dirty glove and raised his hand close to his face. He couldn't see anything. He felt for wetness which would indicate bleeding. Thank God, his finger was dry. The last thing he needed was a trip to the hospital and explaining to Mandy how he injured himself.

From time to time, Woody glimpsed to the left and to the right. The large oak trees blocked his vision. The possibility of someone or something hiding behind one of the trees heightened his anxiety.

Woody halted, listened, and whispered, *"What was that?"* His imagination was playing tricks on him. With every move, his senses intensified as he thought about the prospect of getting caught or being seen.

Tension had set in Woody's shoulders and neck. Sweat rolled profusely down his face and back. His heart rate began racing similar to when he ran on a treadmill.

The crouched position caused cramping to the back of his legs and his knees ached. To give his legs a rest, he changed positions and got down on all fours. He began crawling like a toddler, but he was tiring. Inch by inch, he plugged along as he meticulously placed every nail in the ground until they were all gone.

###

During the day, the binoculars were great, allowing Cee to see things in the distance, but at night it was more difficult. She squinted.

"What's that crawling on the golf course?" Patiently, Cee watched and waited.

"Oh my God! Les, Les. Get the gun."

Les rushed out onto the lanai without the gun. "What's going on?"

Cee handed Les the binoculars. "I know it's hard to see, but take a look at the golf course. Tell me what you see?"

Adjusting the binoculars, Les noticed a large object crawling on the golf course.

"What do you think it is? Could it be the black bear that was mentioned on the nightly news?"

"I'm not sure. It's hard to tell if it's an animal. Let's not take a chance, call the police."

Cee picked up the phone and was dialing when Les stopped her. The large object had turned slightly towards him.

"That's no animal. It's human."

CHAPTER 28

After crawling to the edge of the golf course, Woody stood upright. He began walking, praying he was headed in the right direction. He was excited that his mission was a success, but relieved it was over.

Slowly, Woody walked. From time to time, he glanced at the yards to see if he recognized a house or yard ornament, indicating that he was headed toward his house. After several minutes, he relaxed as he began to notice some familiar landscaping.

Smiling, Woody picked up his pace. After safely returning to his lanai, his breathing was more even and his heart rate had returned back to normal. Inside the lanai, he sat down and shoved the hood off his head. Woody reached for the bottled water he had left on the table.

Slowly, Woody drank the cool water and reflected on what had worked with his plan and what had not. Wiping the sweat off his forehead, he swore he would be better prepared the next time he went out on the golf course now that he knew what to expect.

With the last swallow of water, Woody grinned, stood up and walked into the house. He was proud of what he had accomplished. *"This was his first effort to protect his golf course property."*

When Amanda arrived home, Woody didn't greet her as usual. Hearing the sound of running water, she wondered why he was showering so late.

Kicking off her high-heeled shoes, she headed to the kitchen. Her feet ached and she was both tired and hungry. Before opening the refrigerator door, she washed her hands.

Stepping out of the shower, Woody heard a noise. "Mandy! Is that you?"

"Yes. It's me, Woody. I'm in the kitchen."

After putting on a T-shirt, a pair of shorts, and slippers, he joined her. Before he entered the kitchen, he watched his beautiful wife from the doorway. Walking over to her, he planted a kiss on her neck and held her tight from behind. She turned and gave Woody a deep kiss.

Mandy eased out of his embrace. "Do you want me to warm you up...."

"Isn't that what you've been doing to me?"

Playfully, she hit him. "Do you want something to eat?"

He teased, "If all you're offering is food, then yeah, I'll have some of those chicken wings."

Amanda warmed up the chicken, took the plate from the microwave and placed it in front of Woody. "What did you do this evening?"

Woody would like nothing better than to tell Mandy the truth, but he couldn't and wouldn't. The last thing he wanted was a scolding from her. After all, she was a DA and according to the law, he had just committed a crime.

He avoided making eye contact. "I watched television, but nothing was on. I'm sick of re-runs." He was rambling. "Most of the evening, I sat on the lanai. I enjoyed the view until it grew dark and the mosquitoes thought I was their main appetizer, main course, and dessert."

"I'm sorry I had to work late."

"No problem. I know you have a demanding schedule, especially when you're preparing for a trial."

Amanda was taking aback. This was the first time Woody had appeared understanding about her job. She wondered what was causing the change.

"What are you working on that made you late?"

"A murder and it's a horrendous case. A woman killed her mother because she didn't like or want the responsibility of caring for an aging parent."

Woody shook his head. "What is this world coming to?"

"I know. It's really sad. Not to change the subject, but this case might cause me to work late at least three times a week. I'm really sorry."

Instead of Woody's displeasure, she heard him say, "No

problem, I understand."

"Since I'll be working late, how about taking me to lunch?"

"I have a better idea. Why don't I fix us a picnic basket? If you take a late lunch, it would seem more like having an early dinner for both of us."

Woody was hiding something, but for now, she wouldn't pursue it. She didn't want to spoil the evening. Since Woody had confronted her about her infidelity, she welcomed the times when neither of them were on the defense.

Amanda was still concerned about his health. Since his stroke, she understood the importance of minimizing his stress level.

"Woody that would be fun. I'll call tomorrow morning and let you know the exact time when I can go to lunch."

After they finished dinner, Amanda announced, "I'm going to bed. I have to get up early tomorrow."

"I think I'll join you."

Tonight, Woody was full of surprises and continued to catch Amanda off guard. His routine was to stay up and come to bed after the eleven o'clock news was over.

Amanda took off her clothes and walked into the bathroom. Woody was on the bed, glancing through a magazine. When the bathroom door closed, he put the magazine down and jumped off the bed.

Tiptoeing, Woody hurried across the room to the walk-in closet. He rifled through the dirty clothes hamper and found the only piece of clothing he was interested in—Mandy's under pants.

Woody turned the black lacy panties inside out and raised them to his nose and sniffed. The only scent present was Mandy's. His habit of smelling her panties was not an exact science. However, he prided himself in being able to detect the musty scent of a male and more specifically, sex.

CHAPTER 29

After months of contemplating what to do, the homeowner was ready. The only missing element was a response from the worker. Taking precautions, the homeowner went to the Post Office daily, but what he was waiting for had not come. It was possible that what he wanted might never come.

###

Before the golf course worker, Lee Rogers decided whether or not to accept the mystery envelope job offer, he wanted more information. Unfortunately, the only thing he knew was a name, C.J. Smith and a post office box number.

For several weeks, Lee sat in his car outside the Post Office, watching and monitoring the post office box to see if he could identify C.J. Smith. He spent hours observing the post office box, but no one had approached it. Then again, he didn't know who he was waiting for since he didn't know if his mystery person was a man or a woman.

Lee's efforts had been unsuccessful in finding out more about C.J. Smith and the job offer. The message stated that he had two weeks to reply. His time was running out.

When Lee first retired, money wasn't an issue and he was living comfortably. Then without warning, his company sent him a surprising letter. His health benefits had been cut. His only solution was to get a part-time job that would provide him with health benefits and that is what he did.

He didn't mind working at the golf course. No one bothered him and the early morning schedule allowed him the freedom to do whatever he wanted the rest of the day. He only worked a three day work week at the course.

Lee couldn't help but be suspicious of the job offer, but the money would help him pay off bills and have enough leftover to put into savings. Despite Lee's reservations, he sent a letter according to the instructions to C. J. Smith.

The initial letter didn't state what he would be doing but whatever it was, Lee hoped it wasn't anything illegal.

###

The time was up and the homeowner had not received a reply from the worker. Before the homeowner canceled the post office box, he opened it up. Excited, the homeowner had received the message he had been waiting for.

CHAPTER 30

The worker received his first instructions. Since he had no way of contacting the C.J. Smith, he did as he was instructed. It took Lee two weeks, before he could report his progress.

The letter Lee sent to the post office box stated the following:

Dear C.J. Smith,

As instructed, I have purchased the 5,000 golf balls from the Internet, flea markets, and other vendors. I did not buy more than 100 balls at a time."

In addition, when I bought golf balls at the flea markets and golf shops I wore a baseball cap each time, pulled down low so that my identity was concealed.

Lee

The homeowner received the first progress report and was pleased. The worker had followed all the instructions without question. To the homeowner's surprise, the worker had signed his name.

Now that the homeowner knew the worker could be trusted, it was time for the next step of the plan. The homeowner left another envelope with another payment and the following instructions:

Dear Lee,

Please find your second payment along with enough money to buy daffodil bulbs and baking soda. Do not buy them all at the same location and do it over several weeks.

After all the bulbs have been purchased, combine them with baking soda and water. Make sure you wear rubber gloves when mixing the solution. Place the golf balls in the mixture for twenty-four hours and then spread them haphazardly throughout as many golf courses in The Villages as possible.

C.J. Smith

Lee followed the instructions to the letter. He chuckled when he was spreading the golf balls and repeated what was on the paper. *"Come one, come all, pick up a brand name golf ball."*

Aimlessly, he threw the golf balls in the rough, in the bunker, and along the fairway and golf cart path. He didn't know exactly what the daffodil bulbs and baking soda would do and he didn't want to know.

CHAPTER 31

When Mandy was ready to leave for the office, she kissed Woody. "Don't forget about our lunch date. "

"I won't and don't you forget to call me about the time." As Mandy started to leave, Woody asked, "You're not going to eat breakfast?"

Amanda knew that one of Woody's joys was having breakfast with her before she went to work. With apprehension, Amanda replied. "I'll grab something at work."

She glanced at him and waited for the pouting and pleading for her to sit down and eat something. Instead, she heard, "Have a good day and I'll see you later."

Woody watched Mandy pull out of the driveway and waved. He walked back to the kitchen and cooked breakfast. While eating, he scanned the morning newspaper from front to back, reading every article. To his disappointment what he was searching for was not there. Maybe it was too soon and it was possible that no one had reported a flat tire.

After cleaning the kitchen he walked to the bedroom and stepped on the treadmill for his thirty minute walk. He had fifteen minutes left of his workout when the phone rang. It was Mandy confirming their lunch date. Woody returned to the treadmill, smiling. He was looking forward to spending quality time with his wife.

Woody finished exercising, took a shower and after dressing, decided to make good on a promise he had made to the guys he had taken golf lessons with. The last time all of them were together they talked about how much they missed not golfing on Sundays. Woody could kick himself for volunteering to plan a golf outing for them. He glanced at the clock on the dresser. He had plenty of time to call some of the guys before picking Mandy up for their date.

Hanging up the phone, Woody smiled. Woody was especially happy that he did not have to see Lenny Harper again. He was the man who had an affair with this wife. The last

time they saw each other, Woody had sucker punched him.
   Then there was Donnie Wilson who was a homosexual. He didn't care about his bedroom preferences as long as he didn't have to hear about it.
   Well, none of that was important because no one was available to golf except for Justin Williams, his friend and confidant.

CHAPTER 32

Outside the courthouse, Woody picked up Mandy. As she climbed in she gave him a kiss. She could not help but notice his upbeat mood.

For weeks, Woody had been in an unusually cheerful, positive frame of mind. She was curious as to what was causing the change, but had not found a way to question him about it.

"What have you been doing so far this morning?"

Enthusiasm filled Woody's voice. "I've had a busy morning. After I exercised I called all the guys from the Sunday golf group. I had promised to set up a golf outing for us. Unfortunately, Justin is the only one available on the day that I had scheduled."

"I'm sorry."

"Don't be. This way I can catch up with Justin and since he's usually in touch with all the guys, he can bring me up to date about everyone."

Woody turned into Harris Lake Park and pulled into a parking space. He came around to the side of the car and opened the door for Amanda. When she climbed out of the car, she gave him a tight hug and kiss.

"What's that for?"

"Nothing, I'm just happy that you're getting back to doing the things you enjoy."

They found a park bench overlooking the lake. He sat the basket down and pulled out the tablecloth, placing it on the table. Amanda helped as she took the placemats, plates and silverware out of the basket.

Since Woody shared his news about the golf outing, he had become quiet. As Amanda took a bite of her sandwich Woody broke the silence.

"By the way, I did invite Lenny." She gulped, almost choking. Woody slapped her gently on the back.

"Are you okay?"

Amanda nodded her head.

Woody handed her a bottle of water. "Here, drink." He watched her, examining her reaction.

Amanda wasn't sure what to say. The subject of Lenny was still fresh like an open wound. She hoped Woody would talk about something else.

"I was surprised he agreed to come until he remembered he had another commitment."

An awkward silence hung in the air. Amanda sipped more water. She sat the bottle down, lowering her eyes. When she raised them, Woody's stare was piercing, making her uncomfortable. She broke the silence by changing subjects, telling Woody about the case she was working on.

Their lunch ended too soon, Amanda wished she could take the rest of the afternoon off, but with her workload that was impossible.

Woody drove Amanda back to work and before she climbed out of the car, she reminded him. "I will be working late tonight."

Woody waved good-bye and drove off. Before going back home, he stopped at Home Depot. Woody wanted to find something other than nails to make his night time operation easier.

The reason he had selected nails in the first place was because of his research. From all accounts, the nails should have caused damage without much effort. With each visit to the golf course, it had become easier, but pushing nails into the ground was too time consuming and risky. Besides, there had been nothing in the newspaper about golf carts and flat tires so he wasn't even sure if the nails had worked.

Woody entered the store, searching for a nail substitute. A young store clerk approached him.

"May I help you, sir?"

"Well, young man, I'm looking for something that would cause a flat tire besides nails?" From the clerk's expression, Woody thought how stupid did that sound.

"I should explain. Recently, I had a flat tire and when it was repaired, I guess I was having a senior moment because I forgot to ask what caused it."

"I see. Well, a flat tire isn't always caused by a nail. May I ask where you live?"

"Why?"

"If you live in The Villages a large screw might have caused the flat, especially if you live where there's construction going on. Screws can cause more damage than a nail. All you have to do is drive over a screw and bam, a flat tire is almost guaranteed."

Woody wanted to kiss the clerk. "Thanks. I appreciate your help."

When the young man walked away, Woody found a small basket and purchased five hundred large screws. On his way back home, he wondered if he should have bought more.

With Mandy working late, Woody would be going out on the golf course. Tonight, he would be better equipped than previous nights.

As Woody pulled his polo-shirt off, he heard the door open. "Mandy, is that you?"

"Yes, Woody, it's me."

He put his shirt back on and walked into the kitchen. He gave her a quick kiss. "What are you doing home?"

"I thought you would be happy to see me home early."

"I am. I am. It's just that I'm surprised."

Amanda eyed him and was curious as to what was really going on. Something was wrong and so far she had not been unable to figure it out.

"Come here." Woody looked into her eyes. "I have just what you need to make you relax."

Mandy batted her eyelashes. "What might that be?"

"What about me giving you a massage?"

"That sounds good."

Woody grabbed her hand and led her to the bedroom. She undressed and Woody began working his magic on Mandy's tense muscles."

CHAPTER 33

Equipped with binoculars, Cee sat on the lanai, trying to see her mystery person. Slowly she turned to the left, to the right, and finally focused on the center of the golf course.

"Have you seen anyone on the course?" Les asked.

"No. There has been nothing, zilch! I can't tell you how disappointed I am. It's been quiet except for the nighttime critters. I'm sure the person has been out here, but we probably missed him."

Cee lowered the binoculars and wondered if Les might have been right and that the person they spotted was actually one of the golf course workers. She considered it and dismissed. No, that person was up to no good.

"It's getting late, do you want to go in?"

"Yeah, I guess so." She continued to sit. "Les, did you think of anything we might do about the golfers?"

"I have, but I haven't come up with anything that would change the behavior. Why, did you?"

"Not really, but I'm coming up with some ideas."

"I hope it's nothing that could land you in jail or something that would hurt someone."

Cee waves her hand. "Les, please. I would never do anything illegal or anything that would put us in danger."

Les looked closely at his wife, trying to determine if she was telling the truth. One of the real reasons he had encouraged their earlier move was because of Cee's latest stunt. He had no proof and he never questioned Cee, but he knew she had been the one who had set the fire in their neighbor's backyard. She wanted to prove that the woman had babies living with her which was against The Villages' rules.

Cee was strong willed and determined to a fault. Once she made her mind up about someone breaking the law or doing something wrong, she would stop at nothing to get to the truth.

Les chose his words carefully. "Cee, I love you, but you haven't forgotten the role you played regarding the men who had burglarized the villas."

"Les, Les. I had to do something. The police had given up on catching the thieves because the robberies had stopped."

"I know, but you did take a risk when you pretended to be senile for weeks and left your keys and wallet in a place where the men you suspected of committing the robberies would find them."

Cee raised her hand. "Listen, I did what I had to do to keep the neighborhood safe. At no time were we in danger. The minute I spotted the men in the backyard, I called the police. Didn't the police arrive before the men could break in?"

"Yes, but…." Les stopped. No matter what he said, Cee would never admit that what she had done was dangerous.

"You may not agree with me, but our neighbors like having someone a little nosy living next door to them. I'm as good as having a burglar alarm system."

CHAPTER 34

Lieutenant Wong had waited for this day. However, the call would be bitter sweet.

To finally tell Mr. Kindle that an arrest had been made was like eating apple pie ala mode.

Dan made the call. He had been placed on hold and was waiting for Mr. Kindle to answer. The tip line and the reward had been a God sent. If it had not been for the call, he had no idea when they would have apprehended someone. At this point, it didn't matter. Dan was glad it was over.

Most of the residents as well as the police had suspected that the clubs might have been taken by teens visiting their grandparents. This theory was based on the fact that many of the clubs had been stolen on the weekend. Then, there was the notion that a disgruntled employee must have been responsible.

Dan's thoughts were interrupted. "What's up Dan? I hope you have some good news to report."

"Yes sir I do, but I would rather tell you in person. Is there a good time we could meet?"

"Uh…not really, I'm rather busy today. What's so secretive that you can't tell me over the phone?"

"Well…."

"I don't like games and vagueness. As I mentioned, my schedule is full today. You can tell me whatever it is on the phone."

Taking a deep breath, Dan answered. "Very well. As you know we had a tip line and a reward for any information leading to the arrest of anyone responsible for stealing the golf clubs."

"Tell me something I don't already know. I don't want to rush you, but could you get to the point."

"Yes sir. We received a tip, followed up on it and we made an arrest."

"Great, so why did you want to meet with me?"

"Well…this is not easy."

Impatience filled Mr. Kindle's voice. "Please, spit it out. I don't have all day."

"Your…your two nephews…"

"Wait a minute. Are you saying that my nephews, my sister's boys were the ones behind the stolen clubs?"

"Yes sir. That's why I wanted to tell you in person."

"Where are they now?"

"They're being held at the Marion County Annex. I thought you might want to see them before they're processed."

"How did you know it was them?"

Dan didn't know how much he wanted to tell Mr. Kindle. "Well, the tip we received stated that two men were at the USA Golf Store on County Road 466, trying to trade in a set of golf clubs. I sent two cars to check it out and there they were."

The phone was so quiet that Dan thought Mr. Kindle had hung up. "Are you still there sir?"

"I'm here. Has my sister been notified?"

The so called *"boys"* were over twenty-one so why would he notify their mother. The only reason Dan called him was because he understood the pecking order of things.

"Sir, you're the first one I notified about the arrest."

CHAPTER 35

Not a single article in the newspaper mentioned anything regarding damaged golf carts. This had caused Woody some anxiety. Had the risks he had taken been for nothing? With nothing reported, he was eager to spread the screws over the golf course to see what would happen.

Unfortunately, Mandy had hindered his plans by not working late. As much as Woody tried to appear pleased, he came across as being annoyed and Mandy brought it to his attention.

"Woody, what's wrong? I thought you would welcome me being at home working instead of at the office. Is everything okay?"

Woody's words were harsher than he intended. "Everything is fine. It's just that you might be home, but after dinner you retreat to your home office and work. So, why not stay at the office and work?"

Amanda thought, "Now, that sounded more like Woody." Maybe she should be grateful that he was no longer concentrating on finding ways for her to quit her job.

Woody did not miss the hurt look on Mandy's face. He stood up and gave her a hug. "I love you and I do like it when you come home early. Let's go to bed, that is unless you have some work to do."

Amanda had some transcripts to review, but decided they could wait. "Let's go to bed."

Several days later, when Amanda was about to leave for work she announced, "I'm sorry, but I have to work late tonight." They kissed and she left.

Woody wanted to shout, "Halleluiah." At last he could resume his activities.

To make sure Mandy was not coming home early, Woody waited until eight o'clock.

Before going to the bedroom to change his clothes, Woody looked out the window. According to the weather forecast, it was supposed to rain. If it was going to rain, he'd better hurry.

Quickly, he changed into his black attire. Along with throwing screws on the golf course, Woody had also found something to solve the problem of him not being able to see in the dark. The idea came to him when he learned about night golf.

He bought golf balls and sticks that glowed in the dark. During the day, he acted as if he was doing yard work. Instead, he was placing the golf balls and sticks strategically in various locations in the yard and along the golf course fairway.

Before Woody stepped out the lanai door, he glanced in the direction of where he had placed the glowing objects. Everything was working as planned. The illumination from the balls and sticks was just enough light that he could see the fairway in clear sight.

CHAPTER 36

Like most evenings, Les and Cee were sitting on their lanai, enjoying the balmy weather. Les was just as curious as Cee about the person who had been out on the golf course. Since that first night they had either missed the person or whatever the person was doing it was a onetime occurrence.

Les noticed that Cee wasn't looking out onto the golf course. "What's wrong? You've given up on the mystery person?"

"Every night I've been looking for the person, but I have to agree with you, it was probably a fluke. Besides we don't really know what the person was doing. I guess I was wrong about the person seeking revenge against the golfers."

Les handed her the binoculars. "Go ahead, take a look. This might be the night."

Cee raised them and saw nothing until she stared along the edge of the golf course. "Les, I think we're in luck. Here take a look."

Les saw it too. "Did you notice the person is walking upright tonight instead of crawling on all fours?"

"Yes, I did. Maybe this is a different person."

###

Tonight was a different experience for Woody as he made his way out onto the golf course. Even the darkness seemed friendlier and not so menacing. What a relief not to be down on all fours, pushing nails into the ground, crawling around blindly.

The other nights had taken a toll on Woody's body. For several days, his neck, shoulders, and back were sore and ached.

The Home Depot clerk had given him renewed hope in carrying out his plan. Slowly, Woody strolled along the golf course. Taking his time, he threw the screws in every direction.

###

Cee lowered the binoculars. "I've lost the person."

"Look along the edge of the golf course. Remember, the person is standing up and not crawling around."

"Yes, yes. I see him."

"What makes you think it's a man, Cee?"

"For one thing the person is at least six feet tall with broad shoulders. Here take a look."

Les looked. "I think you're right. It is a man."

The glow balls and sticks were growing dim. When Woody could no longer see their illumination, he stopped and decided not to venture any further onto the golf course.

Before heading home, Woody raised his right hand to throw the last of the screws and stopped in mid-air. A prickling sensation ran up and down his left arm. Gently, he rubbed it, trying to ease the pain.

Another sharp twinge attacked Woody's arm as he began to take a step. The stinging caused him to tread slowly, making his way home. Sweat cascaded down the sides of his face. His heart was beating rapidly and his breathing had become uneven and heavy.

Rather than stop, Woody placed one foot in front of the other, taking it at a slow pace. Reaching the house, Woody was relieved when he opened the lanai door. He whispered, "Thank God."

Woody sank down in the cushioned chair, putting his head back. He took deep, quick breaths and closed his eyes. As swift as the attack happened, the pain had ceased, but there was a throbbing on the left side of his face causing his head to ache.

CHAPTER 37

Since the golf club bandits had been arrested, the Marion County Sheriff Department's activities had returned to normal. Dan was about to leave for lunch when he decided to call his buddy, Roger, the Lieutenant at the Sumter County Sheriff Department.

"Hey, Roger. How's it going?"

"I'm fine Dan. How's everything going with you?"

"Everything is okay. How's the wife and kids?"

"Hey, before we start chatting, let me congratulation you on arresting the golf club robbers."

"Yeah, it seemed like forever, but we caught them. The only thing that was difficult was that they were the developer's nephews."

"So I heard. How did that go down?"

"Not well, but with his money I'm sure they won't spend a day in jail. Anyway, I was calling about another matter."

"What's going on?"

Roger heard Dan exhaled noisily. "For days, the Nancy Lopez Golf Course has been plagued with golf carts getting flat tires and...."

Interrupting Dan, Roger was curious. "Were there that many?

"Well, the department wasn't notified until there had been ten golfers that reported flat tires. At first, the pro shop said the flats might not have happened on the golf course and that's why it took so long for them to call us."

"Now I know why you're calling. You want to know if we've had any flat tire incidents in Sumter County."

Dan laughed. "Well, have you?"

"No. Not that I'm aware of, but if we do I'll be sure to call you."

Before Roger hung up, he had a thought. "Could the nephews be involved in this? You know as retaliation."

They never crossed Dan's mind as suspects. He figured they

had been in enough trouble and wouldn't want to be a part of this. Then again, with those two, you never know.

"You might have a good point, especially since they're out on bail. Thanks for your help and if anything happens in your county be sure to give me a call so we can coordinate our efforts."

CHAPTER 38

In the morning, Woody mulled over last night and the question was whether he should stop. He touched his left arm. The pain he had felt when throwing the last few screws was still fresh in his mind. As much as he wanted to forget, he couldn't. His head ached as if someone was playing drum sticks against his head.

Woody's eyes were closed as he reached across the bed for Mandy. The bed was empty. Where was she?

Slowly, Woody climbed out of bed and took a shower. After drying off, he put on a pair of shorts and a shirt and walked into the kitchen to the aroma of freshly brewed coffee.

Mandy was at the breakfast counter working on her laptop. Her fingers were flying across the keyboard.

Woody's voice was gruff. "You're up early?"

Amanda stopped and peeped up from the laptop. "Good morning to you too," she responded. "Coffee's ready."

"I'm sorry. Good morning."

Amanda jumped down from the bar stool and poured Woody a cup of coffee.

"Has the Daily Sun arrived yet?"

"I don't know. I'm trying to finish this report I need for my morning meeting."

Woody took a sip of coffee, put the cup down on the counter and walked outside. He picked up the newspaper from the driveway and glanced around. The day was going to be a scorcher. The air was hot and muggy and it wasn't even seven o'clock.

When he walked back into the house, Mandy was in the shower. Woody glanced at her computer. The words on the screen confirmed what she had said. She had been doing work.

With the cup of coffee in his hand, he walked out onto the lanai and sat in his favorite chair. Since his accident, he no longer had to worry about golf balls hitting him in the head. With a threat of a lawsuit, Jones not only apologized for the delay, but they enclosed the lanai in acrylic at no cost.

Woody sipped the coffee and closed his eyes. His mind was on the next step of his plan. If Amanda worked late, he would go out again. If she came home on time, he would have to wait.

Mandy yelled, "Woody, I'm about to leave for the office."

Woody opened his eyes, stood up and walked inside. "You're not going to eat breakfast?"

"I don't have time. I'll grab something at work."

"Okay." They kissed and before she left, he asked, "Are you going to work late today?

"I'm not sure, but as soon as I know, I'll call."

"Okay. Have a nice day and don't work too hard."

Woody scrambled two eggs and toasted two slices of wheat bread. He put the food and a glass of orange juice on a tray and walked back to the lanai. Before he started to eat, he opened up the newspaper.

Quickly, Woody scanned every page, but he didn't see what he was looking for. He went back to the front page and read every column carefully, to make sure he didn't miss anything. Before he took another bite of toast, he spotted the article.

CHAPTER 39

Carefully, Woody read every word.

ACCIDENT OR CRIME?

The Sheriff's Department is investigating five incidents of flat tires reported by golfers. Allegedly, the flats happened at the Nancy Lopez Golf Course. The Sheriff did not have enough information to determine if the cause was accidental or acts of vandalism.

Woody smiled and mumbled, "Mission accomplished."

###

Les and Cee were reading the morning newspaper. When Les finished the sports page, he reached for the local section.

"Honey, listen to this." Cee gave him her attention. "The Sheriff's Department is investigating five incidents of flat tires reported by golfers. Allegedly, the flats happened at the Nancy Lopez Golf Course. The Sheriff did not have enough information to determine if the cause was accidental or acts of vandalism."

Les looked at Cee. "Do you think the man we spotted on the golf course is the one responsible for this?"

"Of course he is. I told you that whatever he was doing had to involve the golfers. What a great idea! He thought outside the box when it came to sending the golfers a message about trespassing on private property."

"Do you really think the golfers will get the message?"

"I don't know. I do know you have to try and that's what this man did. My hat goes off to him and now I'll be using my creative juices to think of ways to send a message."

"Like what?"

Cee responded with annoyance lacing her voice. "I don't

know, Les. I'm just saying that this man was clever and I feel a renewed energy in thinking about how I might do something similar."

CHAPTER 40

Later that day, Amanda called Woody as she had promised. "Hi, Honey. I called to say that I'll be working late."

"That's great." Woody could kick himself. "What I meant was, how late will you be working?" He bit his lower lip. That wasn't what he meant. He needed to keep quiet.

Amanda could not help but notice Woody's reaction when she needed to work late. In the past, he would have been furious and upset with her for days. Lately, he seemed almost excited about her working late. She knew her husband too well and he wasn't capable of making such a drastic change unless he was benefitting from it in some way.

"I'll probably be at the office until nine o'clock which means I won't be home until around 10."

Instead of Woody protesting, she heard him say before hanging up. "Don't work too late. I'll see you later. I love you."

To alleviate her worries, she checked his emails and cell phone, but found nothing to indicate what Woody was up to. Her husband had made a complete turnaround regarding her job and her working late and she wanted to know why. She should have been happy about the change, but instead she was distrustful and prying.

The last thing she wanted to consider was the possibility that Woody was having an affair. She knew he had a vindictive side to him. She wouldn't be surprised if he had decided to get even with her for having an affair.

Amanda gave it serious consideration. With her long hours, he had plenty of opportunity. Woody could catch a woman's attention. His body was slender, his arms and legs muscular and his hair was full with striking gray at the temples.

With lots of idle time on his hands; he would have no problem seeking out the company of other women. To make matters worse, there were a large number of women anxious to have male company, even if the men are married.

Her single female co-workers told her that as they grew older they didn't mind sharing a man. Some indicated that they were more interested in companionship rather than the headache of commitment or marriage.

One woman stated, "The advantages outweighed the disadvantages when it came to dating a married man."

Amanda was intrigued hearing this and asked why. The woman was vocal with her explanation. "My husband retired from the military and if I remarry, I'll lose his health benefits."

Another woman said, "My divorce states that if I remarry I lose my husband's pension as well as his social security."

The last woman let out a heavy sigh. "When I was contemplating marriage after my husband died, I wasn't concerned about health and pension benefits, because I have my own. My issue was his adult children. They were afraid I would spend all of their father's money, therefore eliminating or reducing their inheritance."

The first woman asked Amanda. "Now, do you understand why we don't mind dating a married man?" Amanda said nothing.

"We can have companionship and sex, without worrying about the decisions of getting married. It's a win-win situation."

The women laughed, but Amanda found no humor in what they were saying. She remembered reading somewhere that in The Villages there was one man for every ten women. Despite how disturbing the women's statements were, Amanda realized there was probably more truth to what they were saying than she wanted to believe.

CHAPTER 41

Under normal circumstances, golfers in The Villages liked playing all the golf courses. But lately, many of the golfers were not making reservations at the Nancy Lopez Golf Course. When the residents golfed there, their concerns were more about the possibility of getting a flat tire than making birdies and pars.

Some golfers refused to make a tee time there. Other golfers called the flat tire incidents nothing but a "fluke."

Regardless of the golfers' opinions, the police and golf course staff told people to pay close attention to individuals hanging around the golf course. Most of all, no matter how insignificant, the police and staff were asking golfers to report anything that appeared out of the ordinary.

To help combat the offenses, golf course staff began making early morning and late night rounds on the golf courses where flat tires had been reported. The focus of the surveillance was to spot large numbers of nails or screws that might be on the golf course.

It was unusual, but the police solicited the golf course staff in hopes of solving the crime. Lieutenant Wong gave specific orders.

"We appreciate your help. We just don't have enough police officers to cover all the golf courses in The Villages. If you spot any nails or screws, please put on rubber gloves before picking them up.

Wong held up a plastic bag. "Please put all your finds in one of these. We're hoping by taking this action, a finger print might be found on one of the nails or screws. "Thanks you for your cooperation and help."

All golfers were given the usual golf course instructions before teeing off, along with the Starters giving an added warning.

"If you notice an unusual quantity of nails or screws anywhere on the golf course, please do not touch them. Instead, tell the Ambassador or when you finish golfing tell one of the Starters."

Carefully, Lenny Harper listened. Again, he was golfing in The Villages as Paul Collins' guest. While they waited for the four in front of them to tee off, Lenny asked, "What was that all about?"

"Lately, there have been a large number of golf carts that have gotten flat tires."

"Are they sure the flats happened on the golf course?"

"No one really knows for sure. To help to find the individual or individuals responsible for this, some residents have pulled their money together and are offering a 10,000 dollar reward."

"Are you kidding?"

"I'm serious. But, getting the money will not be easy because it will only be paid if the information leads to the arrest and conviction of the individual or individuals committing the crime."

Lenny shrugged. "Do you think maybe some teenagers are doing this for fun?"

"Maybe, but this could also be the work of a disgruntled worker that was recently fired." Paul paused and repeated what everyone was saying, "No matter who is responsible, they will probably face some stiff consequences. You don't mess with The Villages."

CHAPTER 42

Lenny and Paul stopped talking as they drove toward the first tee box. On the second hole, Lenny hit his ball to the left and Paul's went to the right. Paul drove the golf cart to where they thought Lenny's ball landed.

Paul pointed. "You ball should be over there." Stopping the cart, Lenny climbed out.

"I'm going to go find mine." Paul said and drove off.

Lenny found his ball, along with three balls in the nearby rough. As he bent over to pick them up, Paul yelled. "Did you find your ball?"

"Yeah, I found it." Lenny hit but not before putting the balls in his pants pocket.

When Paul picked Lenny up, he was curious. "What took you so long to hit your ball?"

"I couldn't believe my luck. I found three balls."

Paul chuckled. "I found four. I say we are in luck, especially since we're approaching the hole where we have to hit over water?" He laughed again. "We'll need every last one of these balls."

###

On the eighth hole, two golfers were giddy as they climbed out of the golf cart. They were like little children finding eggs at an Easter Egg Hunt. They shared their good fortune with the other two golfers.

One golfer nodded his head like a bobble doll. "We found three balls a piece." He paused. "Did your balls have white, flaky stuff on them?"

Another golfer taunted. "I didn't notice. Besides, who cares? When you get home, wash the balls off."

While another teased, "If they're too messy for you and you don't want to get your hands dirty, you can give those Nike balls to me."

Everyone laughed. The four golfers finished their round of golf, shook hands and talked about their next golf date.

The one golfer who was concerned about the substance on the golf ball stopped by the Starter's shack. "Excuse me, ma'am."

"Hello. May I help you?"

The golfer read the Starter's name tag. "Hi, Doris. I have something to report."

"What is it?"

The man smirked. "Is there a special occasion or is there a treasure hunt going on and no one told the golfers about it?"

With a perplexed expression, Doris cocked her head to the side. "What are you talking about?"

The golfer hesitated as he glanced over his shoulder and leaned close to Doris. "The other men in my foursome and I found an unusual amount of golf balls on the golf course."

Confusion remained on the Starter's face. "And, what's the question? Or better yet, what's the problem?"

The man tugged on his lower lip. Now that he was stating his concern out loud, he sounded foolish. Why was he overly suspicious about finding the golf balls? After all, it's not every day a golfer is lucky enough to find brand name balls except when going in the water and fishing them out.

The Starter's voice interrupted the man's thoughts. "Sir. Sir, is there anything else?"

The man shook his head. "Nah. I guess I just couldn't believe my luck today."

CHAPTER 43

For several weeks Woody continued executing his plan. Again, he was adorned all in black, ready for another night of golf course mayhem. The screws had worked like magic, damaging tires beyond repair. Actually, they worked far beyond his expectations.

With each nighttime operation, Woody had gained more confidence. However, with the flat tire incidents being investigated, the fear of getting caught had increased.

To alleviate his anxiety, Woody changed his plan. Thoughtfully, he pondered his new direction knowing how risky his mission would be. Instead of walking, he headed out in his golf cart.

The destination was the executive nine-hole golf course, Walnut Grove. Woody glanced around the course and had second thoughts. He didn't like how the houses were situated. The biggest problem was that someone could easily see him. Hesitantly, he climbed out of the golf cart and immediately began tossing the screws over the area.

When all the screws were gone, the muscles in Woody's neck and shoulders began to relax. He climbed into the golf cart, sat down, picked up a towel and wiped the sweat off his face. He leaned forward to put the key in the ignition and pulled back. A pain invaded the left side of his body, causing him to sit back. He closed his eyes, waiting for the stinging to cease. Several minutes later, the severity of the pain was gone.

Cautiously, Woody attempted to insert the key in the ignition again. This time, there was no pain. He smiled, thankful that he could head home.

When Woody pulled into the driveway, he was relieved to have made it home without experiencing any additional discomfort. The pain had not lingered, but the left side of his head was throbbing like a toothache. When he entered the house, he walked to the bathroom and took two Tylenol. After he showered, he sat in his favorite chair and turned on the TV, waiting for Amanda to come home.

###

Amanda left work early. When she entered the house, she found Woody asleep in the overstuffed reclining chair. Tenderly she touched his shoulder. He stirred and glanced up at her and then at the clock. "You're home early. I thought you had to work late."

"I decided that work could wait." She winked and teased, "I have other work I need to take care of." Woody's expression wasn't what she had expected. "Is everything okay?"

"Yeah, everything's okay."

Beads of perspiration formed on Woody's forehead and above his upper lip.

Uneasiness filled his entire body, thinking about how close he had come to being caught.

Hoping to erase Mandy's concerns, Woody tried to sound upbeat. "Hey, I'm glad you came home early." He grabbed her hand and pulled her into his lap.

Woody kissed her deeply. Gently, he pulled away and snuggled her neck. He thought he smelled and tasted liquor. He started to say something, but changed his mind. The alcohol on her breath might have been from a drink at lunch with her boss, co-worker or girlfriend or…." Woody didn't complete his thought, not wanting to think about the possibility that Mandy might have spent her lunch with another man.

CHAPTER 44

When the golfers reached the Par 3 Hole #4 on the Walnut Grove Executive Golf Course, the thump-thump sound could not be ignored by the four golfers. At the tee box, all the golfers climbed out of the golf carts and made an inspection. They walked around the carts, looking for the source of the sound.

One of the golf cart drivers asked, "Did you hear that?"

"Yea, I think you might have run over something."

The driver stopped the cart. "I think you're right." She climbed out of the cart. "I don't see anything." The woman kept inspecting. "Maybe, it was a rock and it's embedded in the tire."

The woman driving the other golf cart said, "You don't think…." Her voice trailed off as she climbed out of the cart and looked at the tires.

"What's wrong, did you run over something too?"

"No, but I was thinking about the Starter's warning. You know. If we find any screws or nails on the fairway."

"Yeah, but he was talking about us finding a large quantity of nails or screws on the fairway. We haven't found any screws or nails and we haven't been on the fairway. In addition, neither cart has a flat tire."

In a huff, the woman approached the tee box. "Fine. Let's continue golfing before we create a backup and receive a warning from the Ambassador about not keeping up the pace of play."

On the last hole, the thump-thump returned. This time, the women found large screws sticking out of the tires and they both had flat tires.

The women finished golfing and drove the golf carts to the parking area. They climbed out of the carts and walked to the Starter's shack. When the women reached the Starter, they were all talking at the same time, pointing to the carts.

The Starter couldn't understand a single word. He held up his hands and shouted, "Ladies, ladies, can I have your attention? Please, one at a time. What's wrong?"

The woman with the Dolly Parton build and striking blonde hair became the spokesperson. "Our golf carts have flat tires that were caused by large screws."

In a soothing voice, the Starter said, "I'm sorry this happened. Thank you for taking the time to report the flats. The police are making every effort to find the culprits."

The Starter paused and added, "I'm sure this is not going to make you feel any better, but two other foursomes ahead of you also reported that they had gotten flat tires caused by screws."

With that said, the women started talking in unison again. They were making comments such as, *"This couldn't be a resident. Why would anyone do this? When the police catch the person, they should be punished like any other criminal."*

The Starter had to speak loud to regain the women's attention. "Excuse me, ladies, but do you know the general area where you got the flat tires?" The question was simple, but the women looked confused. "Do you know the hole you were golfing on when you first noticed that something was wrong?"

Although each woman gave a different location, each of them was confident with their answer. Listening carefully, the Starter shook his head. He was reminded of when he was a police officer and took statements from people describing an incident they had witnessed. Rarely did the versions agree.

The Starter interrupted the babbling. "I apologize, but I'm going to have to ask you all to stay until the police arrive. A report must be filed for every incident."

One woman said, "I'm sorry, but that's out of the question. I'm having Mahjong at my house and I have to leave." She looked at the Dolly Parton look alike. "Besides it's your golf cart and you can tell the police what I know, which is nothing."

CHAPTER 45

Every evening while on the lanai, Les and Cee sat patiently waiting for the mystery man to appear on the golf course. After weeks of watching him, he had suddenly disappeared.

"Les, what do you think happened to the golf course man?"

"I don't know. Why?"

"I thought maybe the next time we see him, we should go out on the golf course and talk to him."

"And, we're going to say what?"

Cee shrugged. "I don't know. It's just that I'm excited and supportive of anyone who is willing to protect what is theirs."

"You still don't know if the person is getting revenge against the golfers or not?"

Cee chuckled. "Why else would a person be out on the golf course at night and concealing their identity?"

Les thought about what Cee had said. "I think the next time we see the man, we should call the police. After all, the man is committing a crime."

The suggestion of calling the police made Cee cringe. Would he call the police on her? This man is what the golf course homeowners needed. Cee was about to argue the point but was stopped by what she saw.

"Do you see those lights?"

Les grabbed the binoculars and looked. "I think someone is in a golf cart." He picked up the phone. "I'm calling the police."

"No," Cee said, "I think whoever it is spotted us because the lights are headed in our direction." They watched as the golf cart slowed and stopped in front of their lanai.

A man climbed out of the cart. "Good evening, folks. I'm Lieutenant Dan Wong from the Marion County Sheriff's Department."

Les took the lead. "Good evening to you. I'm Les Tyson and this is my wife, Cee." They glanced at each other waiting for Lieutenant Wong to recognize them, but instead he asked a question.

"In the last several weeks, have either of you seen anything peculiar on the golf course?"

Cee answered. "To be honest since we've moved on the golf course, we have experienced things that you wouldn't believe. Let me tell you about golfers. They have cursed at us, abused our property by trampling on our bushes and flowers, and have broken our window several times."

Lieutenant Wong was glad it was dark and the Tyson's could not see his reactions. So this was the couple that had filed all the complaints.

Les thought, "I don't think that's what the officer's talking about." Rather than stop Cee, he let her vent until the officer interrupted her.

"Ma'am, I'm out here because there have been a number of golfers who have received flat tires while golfing on this course. Have you seen anyone that has been out on the golf course late at night?"

Les glanced at Cee. Neither one of them offered information they had regarding the man they had seen on the golf course.

The officer eyed them and asked again. "Have you seen anything that looked suspicious? You know anything out of the ordinary."

Cee was forceful. "Perhaps if you had taken our complaints seriously maybe someone wouldn't be doing any of this." Les nudged Cee, hoping to silence her.

"Ma'am, are you saying that someone is taking matters into their own hands?"

Cee bit her lower lip. She had questioned enough people to know that she had offered too much information. She took a deep breath. "What I was trying to say is that we have witnessed the rude behavior exhibited by golfers coming onto our property to retrieve golf balls and one homeowner was injured by a stray ball."

Les almost laughed at Cee's rambling. Instead, he began coughing.

"Sir, are you alright?" Les nodded his head. Lieutenant

Wong continued with his questions. "Do you know the name of the injured homeowner?"

"Yes, his name is Mr. Woodward Roberts." Cee pointed. "He lives across the golf course from us."

"How is he doing?"

They both shrugged. Les said, "When it happened, we visited him in the hospital. We haven't seen him since then except for an occasional…. "Les rephrased his response. "What I wanted to say is that Mr. Roberts is our neighbor, we aren't friends or anything."

Lieutenant Wong thanked them. "I appreciate you taking the time to talk to me. Here's my card. If you see or remember anything else please give me a call."

When Officer Wong drove off, he thought that those two knew more than what they were saying. He would bet money that Mrs. Tyson kept an eye on everything that went on in the neighborhood. He made a note to question them at a later date.

CHAPTER 46

The more Woody went out on the golf course, the more satisfaction he had gained from taking things into this own hands. However, the danger had increased with the police now involved and more and more golfers reporting flat tires.

Unlike other nights, Woody had second thoughts. His gut was warning him not to go out, but he changed his mind and decided to go anyway. Putting on his black garb, he headed for the lanai.

When Woody was about to walk out the lanai door he spotted lights. The illumination was off in the distance but close enough for him to see the glow. He wondered, "Was someone else taking revenge on the golfers too?"

Hurriedly, he went back inside, replacing the black T-shirt with a shirt. He rushed back outside onto the lanai. He opened the lanai door and shouted, "Hey! Hey, there!"

The golf cart headed towards the sound of Woody's voice. Within a few feet of the lanai, the cart halted.

"Good evening, sir."

"Hello." In a firm voice, Woody inquired, "What are you doing out on the golf course so late?"

The man answered with a question. "Are you usually on your lanai this time of the evening?"

With caution, Woody replied. "Not really. The golf course is closed and no one should be out here."

"Have you noticed anyone within the last several weeks on the golf course after dark?"

Woody shook his head. "I've heard about some residents playing night golf with glow balls, but I haven't seen them."

"Have you seen any of these late night golfers within the past several weeks?"

"No, I haven't seen them." Woody emphasized, "I've heard about them. Why? What's going on and who are you?"

The man climbed out of the golf cart and approached Woody. "I apologize." Lieutenant Wong extended his hand.

They shook. "I should have indentified myself. I'm Lieutenant Dan Wong with the Marion County Sheriff's Department."

"I'm Woodward Roberts."

"Oh, you're the man who was injured by a stray golf ball."

Woody wondered how Officer Wong knew about his injury. Woody could not be too careful. After all, the man wasn't dressed in a police uniform. "May I see some identification?"

"Yes, Sir." Lieutenant Wong produced a badge and showed it to Woody. Woody examined it, memorizing the badge number, 2478.

"I'll be right back. Wait here."

The officer waited as he watched Mr. Roberts pick up the phone. After dialing the Sheriff Department, Woody walked inside the house when his call was answered.

Woody kept an eye on the man while verifying Wong's information. Woody walked back out onto the lanai.

"I'm sorry, Lieutenant Wong, but I wanted to make sure you were who you said you were. You can never be too careful these days."

"I understand and you should be suspicious. As I asked earlier, have you seen or heard anything suspicious on the golf course within the past several weeks?"

Woody was becoming annoyed. Why did Lieutenant Wong continue to ask the same question? He cautioned himself to keep calm. In a slow, deliberate voice, he responded. "Usually, I don't sit on my lanai this late, but when I saw the lights I became curious."

"What about your neighbors? Are they home?"

Woody's answer was guarded. "I don't really know. They could be out to dinner, at the movies, or playing cards. Who knows? This is The Villages."

The information Woody shared was not true, but he was not about to tell Lieutenant Wong. Recently, there had been a number of police officers that were arrested for breaking and entering into houses while people were not at home.

Officer Wong handed Woody his business card. "If you see

or hear anything, please give me a call."

Again, Officer Wong's antenna was up. Like the Tyson's, Mr. Roberts seemed guarded with his answers. He made a note to find out more about Mr. Roberts' accident and then he would follow-up at a later date.

CHAPTER 47

Amanda had a surprise for Woody. She was going into the office late. She wanted a leisurely breakfast with him, hoping to put some of the spark back into their marriage.

When Amanda entered the kitchen, Woody was busy frying turkey bacon. He did not acknowledge her presence.

"Good morning." Amanda's voice was throaty, giving it a low, sexy sound.

Woody turned his attention to his wife and eyed her. He watched as Mandy took slow, deliberate, model-like moves towards the table before she sat down. A flimsy, white silk gown clung to her body, showing off her curvy hips.

Woody grinned, showing all his teeth. "Good morning. You're not going to work today?"

"I'm going in late. I wanted to spend some quality time with you. Every morning I've been rushing off before we can talk or even have breakfast together. When I come home, from work, either I'm off to bed early or working late on the upcoming trial. Other times, by the time I come home, you're in bed, asleep."

She spread her hands out to both sides of her body. "This morning, I'm all yours."

Woody stopped, turned off the fire under the skillet and pulled her toward him. He gave her a tight hug and then eased his embrace, gazing into her big brown eyes.

"Have I told you how much I love you?"

Amanda wanted to say "no," but didn't. "Yes, and I love you, too."

Woody teased, "We'd better stop this or you're really going to be late for work."

Playfully, Amanda ran her fingers up and down his back. She batted her eyelashes and cooed. "Would that be so bad? Besides, some things are worth being late for."

Amanda did not have to wait for a response. Woody grabbed her hand and led her to the bedroom.

After they made love and showered, Woody dressed and

returned to the kitchen to finish preparing breakfast. When Amanda joined him, she sat at the table, reading the morning paper. "Woody, what do you think about all the golf carts getting flat tires?"

"I don't know. Maybe the same guys that stole the golf clubs are responsible for this too. Who knows? Was something new reported about the flat tire incidents?"

"Um…let me see. The police have concluded that the flat tires occurred on the Nancy Lopez Golf Course or somewhere near the country club."

Casually, Woody said, "Well that would explain why the Sheriff's office had an officer patrolling the golf course last night."

"What? When? You didn't tell me."

"I was already in bed and asleep when you arrived home last night. I'm telling you now."

"What did the officer say?"

He shrugged. "Nothing much. He asked me whether I had seen anyone on the course in the late evening hours. I told him I hadn't seen anything."

Woody placed a platter of scrambled eggs, turkey bacon, and toast on the table. He took a seat across from Amanda.

Woody asked, "What else did the article say?"

"Not too much. The paper has nicknamed whoever is doing this as the Golf Course Menace."

"Well, I still say the police should talk to those two nephews or a teenager or disgruntled employee."

Amanda stopped chewing and said, "You think so?"

Woody put his fork down. "If I were conducting the investigation, that's where I would start."

CHAPTER 48

Four men were golfing on the Oakleigh Executive Golf Course. The men had been in a heated debate since the fourth hole.

By the ninth hole, the robust dialogue had turned into a slight argument. The more vocal golfer said, "I think we should keep our mouths shut. What happened to us might have been a fluke."

Another man in the group added, "What harm would it do to tell other golfers about the golf balls we found or to mention it to the Starter?

The more vocal golfer protested. "Wonder if it's a trap of some sort?"

"What are you talking about?"

"Think about it. This could be connected to the flat tire incidents and this could be a way to catch the guilty parties." The other golfers started laughing.

The vocal golfer's loud voice ended the laughter. "I'm telling you there is more to this than meets the eye. I'm warning you, we need to handle this very carefully."

One of the other golfers responded with confidence. "I disagree with what you're saying. I think one of the workers fished out a large number of golf balls from the water and decided not to keep them." He paused and murmured. "Besides, your theory sounds off-the-wall. What would be the connection between free golf balls and the flat tire incidents?"

The vocal man sighed. "I don't know. It's just a hunch."

Another golfer said, "I can't speak for anyone else, but I feel guilty about keeping the balls. Maybe we should turn them in. We found how many among us?"

No one volunteered how many balls they had found, but one golfer offered, "Although no one is saying, I bet we found at least six apiece." His eyes grew wide. "And to think, they are all brand name balls."

The discussion ended and it was decided to keep quiet about finding the golf balls. When the golfers finished their round of golf they went their separate ways except for two of the guys who rode together. They sat in the parking lot talking for a few minutes.

"I'm curious. The balls you found, did any of them have any white stuff on them?"

"I didn't notice, why?"

"I'm asking because when I picked up two of the balls… some white stuff stuck to my hands and…." The man's voice drifted off and he showed his hands to the man.

"I don't think I had this rash before I picked up the balls." The man paused and hurriedly added, "But then again I have sensitive skin and this rash could be from almost anything."

"Yeah, but if you first noticed the rash after picking up the balls maybe you should have said something to the other guys?"

"Hey, I have no proof that the rash or whatever is on my hands has anything to do with finding the golf balls."

CHAPTER 49

Finally, the golf outing that Woody had planned with Justin had arrived. He was happy they could get together. As much as Woody would have enjoyed golfing with the entire Sunday group he was glad it was just him and Justin. Out of all the guys, Justin had been the one with whom Woody had some connection.

When there are just two golfers, you never know if the Pro Shop will pair you with two other golfers. If that happened it would be okay, but Woody would prefer that it was just him and Justin.

When Woody walked out of the Nancy Lopez Pro Shop, he spotted Justin. He wondered who Justin was talking to. When the man turned around he couldn't believe it. What was Lenny Harper doing here? Had he changed his mind and decided to golf with them after all? If that was the case, he never called Woody.

"Hey, Woody. Look who I found when I parked my car." Justin had his arm around Lenny's shoulders.

"Hi, Woody." Lenny hesitated. "It's been a long time."

Woody wanted to give Justin a hug, but that meant he would….oh no that wasn't going to happen. No warmth was in Woody's greeting. "Hey, Lenny. What are you doing here?" He gave him a limp handshake.

"I know you're probably wondering why I'm here. I'm golfing with a buddy of mind, Paul Collins. He lives in The Villages. At least twice a week we golf together. That's why I turned down your golf invitation."

The tension lifted somewhat as Lenny explained why he was at the golf course. Justin considered how he would feel finding out that his wife had an affair with a guy that he had been taking golf lessons with and had begun to develop a friendship with.

When Justin thought about saying something to relieve the awkwardness of the situation, he heard a man call Lenny's name.

"Hey, Paul." A man greeted Lenny with a friendly hug.

Paul was curious. "I didn't know anyone was joining us today."

"They aren't. These are the guys from the Sunday group I told you about. They're two of the eight that I took my first golf lessons with. Woody Roberts and Justin Williams, this is Paul Collins."

Everyone shook hands and then Paul excused himself. "I need to check in. I'll be right back."

When Paul returned, he exclaimed, "You're not going to believe this, but I arranged for the four of us to golf together."

CHAPTER 50

The last thing Woody wanted was to golf with Lenny, but what could he do? Sarcastically, he said, "This should be an interesting round of golf."

Justin slapped him on the back. "Come on Woody, we're going to have a great time. You'll see."

When Paul and Lenny climbed into the golf cart, Paul was confused. "I thought you guys would have wanted to golf together, but I got the vibe that something's wrong?"

Lenny whispered. "Well, remember when I told you that I had an affair with a married woman."

"Yeah."

Lenny heaved a sigh. "Well, that's her husband."

"What? I'm really sorry man. We can go back and try to change it."

"No, no. It's okay. Besides, Woody invited me to the outing he had planned, until it was cancelled. The time he scheduled it wasn't convenient for anyone."

"Yeah, but I bet he didn't include you to be in his foursome."

Lenny let out a nervous chuckle. "You're right. Let's go. We're next."

The golf round was going at a quick pace. Everyone was hitting the ball straight with only an occasional slice or out of bounds. At the eighth hole, Paul and Justin hit their balls straight in the fairway.

Before Lenny approached the tee box he thought about the first time he had golfed on the Nancy Lopez Golf Course. Sweat began to roll down the side of his face as he swung his driver several times. When Lenny finished his practice swings he addressed the ball and hit.

All the guys watched as Lenny hit the ball. Lenny bit down on his lower lip as he sliced the ball to the right.

Lenny prayed, "Lord, let it come back to the left."

Woody swore under his breath. His nose flared as he enunciated each word. "I think your ball hit my house." Woody squinted and sneered. "To be more exact, your ball might have broken my window."

The other guys gasped. Lenny threw his head back, blew out air, and uttered, "Not again." Involuntarily, the words had escaped and immediately he regretted it.

Woody moved close to Lenny's face, glaring as he exhaled loudly. With attitude he said, "This isn't the first time you've hit my house is it?"

CHAPTER 51

Sweat rolled down the sides of Lenny's face. He blew out a loud breath of air. He cleared his throat.

"Well…the first time I golfed on this course I hit a similar ball, just like today. When Paul and I were having lunch, I…we… learned that a homeowner had been injured by a mishit ball."

Defensively, Lenny threw his hands up. "But, to be honest, I'm still not sure it was my ball that hit the homeowner."

With pursed lips, his jaw taunt, Woody growled, "Oh, it was your ball. I know it as sure as my name is Woodward Roberts."

Childish as it may be, Woody couldn't help but think about Mandy and Lenny's infidelity. He raised his fist, but before he could connect with Lenny's chin, his arm lowered.

Shaking his head, Woody blinked. Bright objects floated in front of his face. His head felt as if it was about to explode and his legs were trembling. When he raised his fisted hand again his body tumbled to the ground.

Everyone rushed to Woody's side. His eyes were fluttering and his words were slurred. He tried to sit up.

Justin put his hand on Woody's shoulder. In a soothing, reassuring tone, he said, "Don't move, man."

Without hesitating, Lenny pulled out his cell phone and dialed 911. "An ambulance should be here shortly. In the meantime, stay still."

Moving away from the guys, Lenny opened his cell phone. He punched in Amanda's phone number.

Lenny chewed the inside of his mouth as the phone rang. "Please pick up, Amanda." He didn't want to leave a message

"Hello, this is Amanda. I can't answer your call. Leave me a message and I'll get back to you as soon as I can. Have a great day."

Lenny whispered into the phone. "Amanda, this is Lenny Harper. Please call me as soon as you receive this message."

Amanda's phone vibrated. She picked it up and glanced at

the number. Her eyes grew wide when she saw Lenny's number. Why was he calling her?

Hurriedly, Amanda finished giving her secretary instructions. "Please close the door on your way out."

When the door closed, Amanda dialed Lenny's number. The second she heard his voice, she lit into him.

"Lenny." Her voice did not hide her anger. "Why are you calling me?"

Delivering bad news is something you don't want to do over the phone and this was one of those times. "There's been…I mean…." Lenny hesitated.

Amanda's anger changed to worry. "What's wrong?"

Lenny cleared his throat. "Woody is being taken to The Villages Regional Hospital."

CHAPTER 52

All weekend, The Villages Hospital had been inundated with men and women coming into the ER. Almost every chair was filled.

A nurse walked out into the waiting room, holding up her hands. "Ladies and gentlemen, may I have your attention. The hospital appreciates how patiently everyone is waiting, but you might be better served if you went to the Leesburg Hospital or to one of the urgent care facilities in the area."

Everyone acknowledged the suggestion, but no one budged. Instead, loud protests were uttered. Some stated that they had driven their golf carts to the hospital and would have to go home and get their car. By the time they did that they probably could have seen a doctor. Others murmured that they had been dropped off at the hospital and had no one to drive them to Leesburg or anywhere else. The remaining individuals stated that they were too sick and didn't want to leave.

With the over whelming number of people coming to the hospital, the doctors, nurses, and other hospital staff were exhausted. They were also worried that with little or no sleep their immune systems could be weakened, making them more vulnerable to whatever was causing the illness.

In an effort to determine any commonalities among the sick individuals, the CDC was analyzing everyone being seen. So far, the information obtained from the forms had only revealed three facts. Number 1: No one was related; Number 2: Not all individuals lived in The Villages; and Number 3: everyone affected was over the age of 40.

Hour after hour streams of people continued to enter the hospital doors. The admission's clerk, a young woman in her twenties, was overwhelmed. The name tag read, Sandy.

The wait for individuals wanting to see a doctor was much longer than any of the sick had anticipated. Sandy was sympathetic, but there was very little she could say to comfort them. The sick as well as the people waiting with them were weary. Tempers were flaring and patience was growing thin.

Sandy was being bombarded with questions: *"When could their loved ones expect to see a doctor? How much longer would it take? Is there something they could be given to ease their pain? Could more chairs be placed in the waiting room?"*

Sandy prayed that the number of sick people walking through the Emergency Room doors would slow down. Unfortunately, her prayers had fallen on deaf ears as another man walked through the doors and approached her.

Sandy smiled and handed the man a clipboard, but before she could give any instructions, the man grabbed his stomach. The man raised his hand, covering his mouth.

Quickly, Sandy jumped up from her chair, managing to avoid the contents of his stomach from emptying out on her desk as well as on her. She was helpless as she watched the man heave uncontrollably. When he appeared to be finished, the man's face was red from embarrassment as he apologized. At that point, Sandy offered him a box of tissues.

Sandy forced a smile. "I understand. Why don't you clean up? When you come back you can fill out the necessary forms."

After assisting the man, Sandy made a call. "I need a custodian in the ER for a cleanup."

Sandy made another call. Within minutes, the head nurse on duty appeared at her desk.

The nurse's voice was full of annoyance. "What's wrong? Your message stated there was an emergency."

"All of these people have similar symptoms and...." She gestured and pointed. "That man threw up and if I had not jumped up it would have been all over me."

Sandy lowered her voice. "Something has to be done. I know everyone is working hard and they're tired, but with people throwing up and running to the bathroom, we don't have enough staff to keep up. We have to do something to combat some of this."

The nurse let out a loud sigh. "I know. I'll be right back." The nurse returned and gave Sandy the following instructions.

"Give each person in the room and anyone else coming in with the flu-like symptoms a barf bag and an adult size diaper.

CHAPTER 53

Dan was tired. It had been a long day and he was glad to be home. After he showered and dressed he had a date with Becky. Their plans were to go to the Old Mill Movie Theater in The Villages. After the movie, they were going to dinner at the Cane Garden Country Club.

While Dan was dressing, the phone rang. "Hi, dad. How are things going?"

"I'm doing fine, but I'm calling about your mother."

"What's wrong with mom?"

"I don't know." Mr. Wong paused. He didn't want to upset his son, but he had to tell him. "I just came back from the hospital."

"Is mom alright?"

"I think so. I'm calling because she's been admitted to The Villages Regional Hospital."

"Why? Is it her heart?"

"No, no. They said she probably has a virus."

Dan must have misunderstood his dad. If it wasn't her heart then why was she admitted to the hospital? His dad wasn't making sense.

"Did the doctor say why mom had to be admitted if it was a virus?"

"No and that's what's crazy. You wouldn't believe how many people are sick from this virus. It was like something out of a movie. With so many people throwing up, I couldn't wait to get out of there."

"Are you okay, Dad?"

"Oh, I feel fine."

"Listen, I'm about to pick Becky up, but before we go to the movies and dinner I'll stop by the hospital."

"I would appreciate that son. Tell Becky I said hello and have fun."

"Dad, thanks for calling and don't worry. Bye."

Dan didn't know what to think about what his dad said

regarding all the sick people at the hospital. And why was his mother admitted if it was only a virus?

CHAPTER 54

When Becky opened the door, Dan couldn't miss the dark circles under her eyes. She noticed how Dan was inspecting her. She indicated that she had been working overtime, but from her face, she appeared as if she needed rest. He said nothing and gave her a kiss.

"Dan, do you want to come in for a minute? We have time before the movie starts?"

"Thanks. When they sat on the sofa, Dan asked, "Are you okay?"

"I'm fine. It's just that I've been working long hours. People have been coming to the hospital by the hundreds."

"I heard."

"How…." She laughed. "I forget you're the police and you know everything."

"I wish. My dad called me just before I came to pick you up. He said that mom has some sort of virus that seems to be going around. Can you tell me why she's been admitted to the hospital just because she has a virus?"

"I don't know what to tell you."

"What do you mean?"

"What I mean is just that. People have been coming to the hospital, all of them sick with flu-like symptoms, but the mystery is the rashes they all have on their hands."

"What are the doctors doing about it?"

"They've called in the CDC. I'm sorry, the Center for Disease Control and Prevention. They are…."

Dan wanted answers. He didn't know if Becky couldn't tell him or she just didn't know any more than what she was saying.

"I'm sorry if I sound impatient, but do they know what's causing this illness?"

"No. That's why they're admitting anyone who has come down with the virus. That way they can monitor it."

"Do you mind if we stop by the hospital before we go to the movies and dinner?"

"No problem." Becky hesitated. "In fact, we can buy take out and come back here and watch a movie."

CHAPTER 55

Les raised the binoculars, scanned the golf course and watched a golfer picking up golf balls. Les thought the man resembled a child at a Treasure Hunt, delighted in finding the prize.

Les smiled and turned his attention to the tee box. He adjusted the binoculars and began yelling. "Cee, Cee. Quick, come here."

She rushed through the open lanai sliding doors. "What's going on?"

He handed her the binoculars. "Look at the tee box."

Her mouth flew open. "Oh my! I wonder what happened."

"I don't know. I was glancing over the golf course when I spotted the man on the ground with men standing around him."

Les and Cee watched in silence, lost in their own thoughts. Cee exclaimed. "I'm not sure, but I think that's Mr. Roberts on the ground?"

Taking the binoculars from Cee, Les zeroed in on the man lying on the ground. "It sure looks like him, but I'm not sure since I can't see his entire face."

"I'm pretty sure it's him." Cee picked up the cordless phone. "I'm going to call 911?"

Les stopped her. "I'm sure someone had a cell phone and has already called."

"I sure wish we knew what happened."

Les lowered the binoculars. "Do you think Mr. Roberts might have had a heart attack?"

"Whatever happened, the EMTs have arrived." Les raised his binoculars, watching as Mr. Roberts was placed on the stretcher and carried off the golf course.

Cee was curious. "I wonder which hospital he's being taken to."

"Since The Villages is the closest I would think they're taking him there."

Excitement was in Cee's voice. "Let's go to the hospital and see what we can learn."

Usually Les discouraged Cee's snooping, but in this case his curiosity had also been peaked.

CHAPTER 56

In less than ten minutes, the ambulance arrived at The Villages Hospital. Justin, Lenny, and Paul sped closely behind the ambulance in their cars. When the gurney burst through the automatic sliding glass doors, Justin, Lenny, and Paul were right behind it.

One of the paramedics turned and spoke to Justin. "You'll have to wait here. Mr. Roberts is being taken to one of the examination rooms. You might want to check in with the Admission Desk and let them know that his wife is on her way."

After Justin checked in at the desk, he joined Paul and Lenny. They were commenting on the number of people in the ER.

"It's a little weird isn't it?" A woman sitting near them interrupted their conversation.

"From what I understand all of these people are here for the same reason." The men looked at her and before any of them could ask she explained.

"Oh, I'm here because of my husband. He was golfing earlier and by the time he came home he had stomach cramps and was vomiting."

No one asked any questions as the woman kept explaining.

"After several hours of him throwing up, I made him come to the ER." The woman gestured with her hands. "You know how you men can be." She let out a slight chuckle.

"When we arrived and entered the ER, we couldn't believe how crowded it was. Of course, my husband wanted to leave, but I made him stay, especially when he began…" Her voice lowered and let out a nervous laugh. "Well, now he's having problems at the other end."

Paul was about to make a comment, but the woman hurried on. "For anyone who's sick, you're given these." The woman held up a white bag. "A barf bag and…." Her face turned red and rather than tell the men, she held up a large adult- size diaper.

When the woman finished, Lenny bent his head over. Before he threw up the woman screamed. "Here, take the bag."

Afterwards Lenny seemed embarrassed. "Thanks." He excused himself and went to the restroom.

"I think your friend might have the same thing as my husband and the others. Here give him this and I'll get my husband another one. I also suggest your friend might want to check in to see a doctor."

Justin went after Lenny. In the restroom, Justin stood near the door. "Lenny, are you okay?"

"I don't know."

"Listen, where are you?"

"I'm in the second stall."

"I'm going to hand you…" Justin walked to the stall and bent down and handed the diaper to Lenny.

When Lenny returned his friends encouraged him to sign in. He protested at first until Justin said, "What's the harm? You're already here and you're sick." Reluctantly, Lenny did as he was told.

Justin stood up when he saw Amanda entering the ER. He approached her with a slight smile. "Hi, Amanda."

"Hi, Justin." Amanda's facial expression was full of concern. "Where's Woody?"

"We were told to wait here. According to the paramedics, he was taken to an examination room."

Justin shrugged. "That's about all we know. Why don't you join us while we wait to hear from the doctor?"

Amanda stood glancing around the room. Justin repeated what the woman had told them. Justin let out a nervous laugh.

"Oh yeah, anyone checking in with a temperature, stomach cramps, vomiting, and diarrhea are given a barf bag and…." Justin whispered, "An adult diaper."

Wide-eyed, Amanda asked, "Is this virus contagious?"

"I hope not because I have some critical work projects I have to finish and more importantly I would hate to take this home to my wife and children."

Justin could tell Amanda was uneasy about his suggestion that she join him. He thought he understood why.

"Uh…this morning it was accidental that Lenny was golfing with us. Since we arrived at the hospital, he's not feeling well. We convinced him to see a doctor. Right now, he's back in the restroom."

Amanda smiled and raised her hand. "Spare me the details."

As Justin weaved through the rows of chairs and stepping over people's feet, Amanda said, "Thanks for everything."

CHAPTER 57

The wait time in the ER to see a doctor had decreased now from over an hour to about forty-five minutes. Despite the shortened wait time, tempers continued to flare, complaints were still being voiced, and frustration was making everyone ill-tempered.

Every time the double oak doors opened, all attention focused on whoever walked through them. This time a man dressed in green and a woman dressed in blue emerged. The man boomed over the loud voices.

"Mrs. Woodward Roberts. Mrs. Woodward Roberts."

Apprehension and tension filled Amanda's body as she approached the doctor. "Hello, Dr. Timmons. How's Woody's doing?"

Dr. Timmons suspended with all the niceties. "He's going to be fine. The palpitations, trembling, and shortness of breath were caused by an anxiety attack."

Amanda let out a heavy sigh. "Thank God. Can I see him?"

"Yes, but the attack suggests that Woody may be under some sort of stress. If he is, he needs to address whatever is going on and get it under control, especially with him having a recent stroke."

Amanda couldn't explain what "stress" was going on in Woody's life because she didn't know. She bit her lower lip and wondered if golfing with Lenny triggered the attack.

Dr. Timmons was staring at Amanda. "Is everything okay?"

"Yes, I was just thinking about what you said. I'll do my best to help Woody reduce his stress. Can I see him now?"

"Yes. In fact, he can go home. Just make sure he gets some rest."

The blue clad woman who had been standing beside the doctor was looking at the chart in her hand. Everyone sat with anticipation, hoping their name was going to be called next.

In a loud voice, she called, "Mr. Lenny Harper. Mr. Lenny Harper."

The nurse showed Lenny to an examination room and took his temperature and blood pressure. The nurse's facial expression was noncommittal about his condition. He watched as she wrote something on the chart she had carried into the room with her. After the nurse finished writing, she exited, saying nothing and taking the chart with her.

Easing down on the examination table, Lenny laid back. From all the throwing up, his throat was sore and his mouth was dry. At least for now, the diarrhea had stopped, but the rash on his hands seemed to be spreading.

Lenny must have dozed off because he didn't hear anyone enter the room. Opening his eyes, he was surprised to see a man standing over him.

"Hello, Mr. Harper. My name is Dr. Jacobs." He glanced at the chart he was carrying and put it down. "Please sit up."

The doctor put on a pair of latex gloves, removed his stethoscope and listened to Lenny's heart. He shined a light in his eyes and asked Lenny to open his mouth as he examined his throat.

Dr. Jacobs wrote something down and asked Lenny a series of questions. Then, the doctor said, "I'm going to have you admitted to the hospital."

Lenny was confused. "Admitted to the hospital? Why? Don't I have a bug of some sort?"

"Well…" Dr. Jacobs pulled off the gloves and didn't look at Lenny as he explained. "This is just a precaution. You and a large number of people are sick with similar symptoms."

In a weak tone, Lenny interrupted Dr. Jacobs. "I don't understand."

"Tests are being run on everyone with these symptoms. Hopefully, the problem can be identified and appropriate treatment can be administered to combat whatever is making everyone sick. As I stated, this is just a precaution."

CHAPTER 58

Les and Cee were disappointed that they could not go immediately to The Villages Hospital. They both had doctor's appointments and could not change them. Their visit to the hospital would have to wait until the evening.

While they waited to see the doctor Cee shared. "Les, living on the golf course is better than watching the daily soaps." They laughed.

"Cee, do you really think the man was Mr. Roberts?"

"Yes, I do."

"What are we going to do if it wasn't Mr. Roberts? How are we going to find out who the man was?"

"I don't know, but I'll think of something."

When Les and Cee walked into the ER, they both halted in their tracks. Cee surveyed the room and whispered. "What's going on in here? If I didn't know better I would think that an epidemic has broken out and no one told the rest of us."

Les laughed. "I wouldn't go that far, but let's go to the main entrance and see if one of your volunteer friends is working the Information Desk."

When Les and Cee turned the corner, disappointment covered their faces. The volunteer sitting at the desk wasn't anyone Cee knew.

Les asked, "Now what do we do?"

Cee didn't answer right away. "Follow my lead."

She walked up to the desk. "Hi." With a quick glance at the woman's name tag, Cee said, "Hi Julie. You probably don't remember me, but I used to work as a hospital volunteer."

Before Julie could respond, the telephone began ringing. She picked it up, raising her finger to Cee, indicating that she would be with her in a minute.

While Cee waited, she glanced around at the level of activity in the Main Lobby. Doctors, nurses and other staff were bustling around in an efficient but hurried manner. Watching them, Cee thought their movements seemed urgent.

Julie hung up the phone and turned her attention back to Cee. "I'm sorry. Now, how can I help you?"

"As I was saying, I used to work here. I was wondering if the hospital...."

The ringing phone interrupted Cee before she could finish her sentence. Cee let out a noisy sigh.

With the telephone back in the cradle, Julie said, "I'm really sorry about the interruptions, but it's been chaotic around here. An unusual amount of people have been coming into the hospital with the flu. What's puzzling is that for some reason these people are being admitted to the hospital." Again, the phone rang and the woman made an apologetic gesture.

Although Cee and Les didn't learn anything about the man, they did find out why there was such a high level of activity at the hospital. Cee grabbed Les's arm.

Considering what Julie had said, Cee murmured. "Cover your mouth and let's get out of here."

Les did what he was told. Outside on the sidewalk, he stopped. "Please Cee, you need to slow down and tell me what's going on."

"Are you kidding me? Didn't you see all those sick people in there? Whatever they have could be contagious or worse, airborne. This could be an epidemic and the hospital is trying to keep it quiet."

"Well, I don't know about that."

"Well I do and..." Cee didn't finish her sentence when she spotted Lieutenant Wong and a woman walking toward them.

"Well, hello Officer Wong." Cee smiled.

"Hello Mr. and Mrs. Tyson." Dan and Becky were about to walk pass them when Cee stopped them.

"Are either one of you sick?"

Dan and Becky looked at each other. "Thanks for asking, but we're both fine. Are either of you sick?"

"Oh no. We were here to see a friend, but with all the people in there we decided it was best we went home before we catch something. Are you visiting someone?"

"Not really." Dan paused. "I'm sorry. This is my fiancé, Becky Summers and she's a nurse."

With raised eyebrows, Cee was curious. "Since you're a nurse, what's going on in the hospital? It doesn't take a police officer or a private investigator to recognize when something is out of the ordinary."

Becky was thrown off guard by the woman's comment. "I...at the present...I..."

Dan took charge. "What's she's trying to say is that a large number of people with flu-like symptoms are being admitted to the hospital, but there is nothing to be concerned with."

Suspiciously Cee eyed both of them and pursed her lips. "I guess that's the story you're telling people and you're sticking to it."

CHAPTER 59

When the Tyson's were far away from Dan and Becky, she asked, "Who was that woman? How do you know her?"

Dan chuckled. "I met her and her husband the other night when I was doing night duty on the golf course."

"If anyone knows anything about those golf carts and flat tires, I would put my money on her. I don't think she misses much in her neighborhood."

"I agree, but according to the couple, they've seen nothing."

Becky laughed. "I wouldn't believe that for one minute."

When they walked into the hospital entrance, Dan was shocked, but tried to remain expressionless. "I had no idea there were so many people sick with this virus."

"I told you that the hospital has been inundated. That was the reason why the hospital decided to have these people admitted until they can figure out what's going on." She lowered her voice. "What people don't know is that everyone with the virus has been isolated to one floor and the rumor is that the hospital is beginning to run out of space."

"Is it safe to visit my mother?"

"So far, the virus doesn't seem to be contagious."

Becky knew Dan's mom was on the third floor, but she had no idea where. When they stepped out of the elevator onto the third floor, it was frightening. Even Becky was surprised. She had not been on the third floor since the hospital started admitting people and had no idea that beds would be lined up in the hallway.

Lucky for Dan, his mother was in a room, but three beds had been cramped into the little room. When they walked in, they had to walk sideways to reach his mom's bed.

Dan was worried. With the floor being so crowded and considering her pre-existing health problems he wondered if his mom was receiving the medical attention she needed.

Tenderly, Dan touched his mom's arm. "Mom."

She opened her eyes. Weakly, she murmured. "Hi, son. What

are you doing here?"

"I'm here to see my best girl. How do you feel?"

Weakly, she answered, "I've had better days. How's your dad?"

For the first time, Dan noticed the rash on his mother's hands. "He's fine. I'm not going to stay long, but I wanted to see you. Dad said he would be back later."

He kissed the top of his mother's forehead. "You need your rest. I'll be back tomorrow. Get some sleep." He and Becky left.

Inside the car, Dan quizzed Becky about the virus, the hand rash, and medical treatment, but her answers did not satisfy him.

CHAPTER 60

After arriving home, Cee was more determined than ever to inform their neighbors and friends about the strange occurrence going on at The Villages Hospital.

Cee was adamant. "People should know that something mysterious is going on and our life could be in jeopardy."

"I agree, but what can we do?"

"There's a lot we can do. For one, our neighbors can start calling the police and the hospital and ask questions about this so call virus."

"Don't you think we need more information before we tell people about this? After all, we don't want to alarm people."

Exasperated, Cee threw her hands in the air. "Excuse me, what more do we need to know? Large numbers of people with flu symptoms are being admitted to the hospital. That's not normal."

Slapping the side of her head with her hand, Cee exclaimed, "I know what's going on. These people are being admitted to the hospital because the doctors don't have a clue as to what's wrong with them. They want to keep them isolated similar to when people had to be quarantined?"

A slight chuckle escaped Les's mouth. "I'm sorry but Cee you're letting your imagination run wild."

"No I'm not. I've watched enough TV medical and police programs to know what's going on. These people have some kind of unidentifiable illness that could be the work of a serial killer or worse a Terrorist. I'm calling the police. A warning needs to be issued."

"Wait a minute. Do you think the police are going to take your word for it?"

"They don't have to. I'll tell them to talk to Lieutenant Wong."

"Why him?"

"Because we saw him at the hospital and he knows more than he was willing to tell us." Cee hurried on. "And, did you notice how antsy his fiancé, the nurse was when I asked her questions about the virus?"

Les shrugged.

Rolling her eyes, Cee exhaled. "You didn't have to notice, but I did. I'm telling you Les, we're in danger and we need to take action."

CHAPTER 61

The much needed rain had been falling all day. Despite the precipitation, Woody was enjoying the view. As he stared out on the golf course he was surprised and pleased that not one golfer had made an attempt to golf.

Woody sipped on his lemonade and thought about his recent attack. He was thankful that it had turned out to be nothing more than an anxiety attack. Another stroke would have devastated Mandy and him. When she asked what was causing his stress, he lied.

The reason he gave her was Lenny. Woody blamed it on the affair. As much as he thought he had put their affair behind them, he now knew that talking and seeing Lenny must have been too much for him.

The real root of his problem was Lenny. If it was not for him, Woody would never have sustained the head injury and despite what the doctor kept saying, he still believed the accident brought on his stroke.

How did a man he detested so much, continue to play a role in his life? The more he tried to get rid of him, the more he kept coming back.

In some ways, he wished he had never found out that Lenny had been responsible for his injury. First Lenny had an affair with his wife and now he was the source of his health problems.

Lenny was like the corn on his baby toe. No matter how many home remedies or store bought ointments he tired, it kept coming back more annoying than when it first appeared.

When Woody was taken to the hospital, he was sure Lenny was busy consoling Mandy. If it happened, he would never know and Mandy certainly wouldn't mention it. He wondered if Lenny told Mandy that he had caused his head injury.

Thinking about Lenny and reflecting on everything made Woody's chest tight. Slowly, he inhaled and exhaled. Closing his eyes, he felt his body relaxing.

Perhaps he was lucky that he had the anxiety attack. Maybe,

he needed to rethink the whole night-time golf course operation. What was the point? Should he continue the revenge plot knowing who had been the source of his injury?

Chapter 62

One of Woody's biggest motivations for living a healthier life was Mandy. Maybe he would start a new beginning by not calling her Mandy. She hated the nickname. On their first date, she asked him not to call her that.

What Mandy didn't know was that he liked the nickname because of the porn star, Mandee. He would never tell his wife, but she and the porn star had similar attributes that most men appreciated. Just thinking about them made his manhood rise.

The stroke and the anxiety attack had given Woody time to think about his life, especially his marriage. If he were to live a long, fruitful life with his beautiful wife, he would have to make some changes.

Another reason, as silly as it sounded; Woody feared that if he died, Mandy...Amanda would take up with Lenny again. How foolish for him to have such thoughts. Once he was dead, he would have no control over what Mandy did or whom she did it with.

A devious thought made Woody chuckle. Since his wishes were to be cremated, he would convince Mandy to wear a locket around her neck with his ashes in it. This way he would always be with her and, the locket, a constant reminder that she once belonged to him.

The ringing phone interrupted Woody's scheming. "Hello."

"Hi, Woody. This is Justin. How are you doing?"

"I'm doing okay for an old man. What about you?"

"I'm fine. I'm not going to take up too much of your time since I'm making calls to all the guys from the Sunday golf group."

"What's going on?"

"I was at the hospital today and wanted to give everyone an update on Lenny."

"What about Lenny?"

"I'm sorry. I thought Amanda...." Justin stopped in mid-sentence and bit his lower lip. "Lenny has that virus that so many people have. He's in The Villages Hospital."

Anger was boiling inside of Woody. "I didn't know. Maybe, Amanda was too worried about me to mention anything about Lenny."

Justin didn't acknowledge Woody's statement. He was surprised however, that Amanda had not told him. But, knowing Woody, he could understand why she didn't.

"How is he doing?" Woody reminded himself that Justin was just the messenger and not the root of his problems. "Can he have visitors?" Woody inquired, but he had no intentions of visiting him.

"First of all, he's not doing well. To answer your second question, the hospital is asking that only immediate family visit those with the virus. I'm exempt because I'm a minister and even then with the new privacy laws, I can only visit those I know by name."

"Why don't the doctors know what's wrong with these people?"

"I'm not sure." Justin wasn't going to spread the latest grapevine gossip about the virus being a new strain or that it could be a work of a Terrorist.

"You're not afraid that the disease is contagious?"

"So far, it doesn't seem to be."

Woody's evil thoughts made him smile. Perhaps Lenny would die from this disease. What a blessing and to think he wouldn't have that thorn in his side any longer.

"Woody, are you still there?"

"I was saying a quick prayer for Lenny." He lied. "When you visit him again, tell him that Amanda and I are praying for his speedy recovery."

CHAPTER 63

Despite Les' pleas, Cee went forward in holding an emergency meeting with their neighbors. As suspected, no one was overly concerned with what Cee had to say. They believed that if there was an epidemic of some sort, the police or the news media would have issued a warning.

After the meeting, Les pleaded. "Cee, honey, maybe the neighbors are right about us over reacting to what we saw. Let's wait and see what happens."

She smirked, "Les, we can't wait. If we do nothing, people could die." She patted him on the hand.

"Come on Les. I have just the plan. I'm sure it will work, you'll see."

The plan called for Cee to buy pay-as-you phones. Cee had watched a Law and Order TV episode that explained how caller ID allowed the police to identify callers as well as trace calls. Another precaution would be for them to make the call in various locations throughout The Villages and of course they would use fictitious names. With everything in place, it was time to implement the plan.

Les made the first of several calls, alternating between cell phones. After the third call, he had lost his confidence.

"The police aren't going to do anything. I could hear the laughter in the police officer's voice when I made the second report."

In a reassuring tone, Cee said, "Don't worry, they will. Here, let me have those phones."

Each time Cee made a call to the Sheriff Department it was difficult for her to disguise her southern accent. With each call, she made a note of the time, location and what she said. This was to help her from getting mixed up.

Cee had an idea that might grab someone's attention. "Hello. My name is Dallas Goodson. I'm calling about The Villages' Hospital. Do you know that half of The Villages' residents have been admitted to the hospital with some sort of strange disease?"

"Ma'am, you've called the Marion County Sheriff Department."

"I know. I'm calling because this could be the beginning of a land attack on the United States by a Terrorist."

Without hesitation, the officer said, "Ma'am, that's a serious allegation. What makes you think this could be a Terrorist attack?"

"With no disrespect, put the dots together. If there are a number of people with an unexplained disease and these individuals are being quarantined, what do you think?"

"Ma'am, do you have any proof in what you're saying? Ma'am, are you still there?"

Cee hung up, smiling. Her point had been made and she had grabbed the police officer's attention.

Les hugged Cee and kissed the top of her head. "Maybe we should contact the newspaper." He paused and grinned. "I have an idea." He took the phone from Cee.

"Hello. I can't give you my name, but I have information about an unexplained disease that may be reaching epidemic level. The sick individuals are at The Villages Hospital."

"Sir, what is your name?"

"You don't need my name to learn more. Just call the hospital or the Lake, Marion and Sumter County Sheriff Departments."

CHAPTER 64

According to the homeowner's information, the plan had been flawless. The golf balls left on the golf course had enticed most golfers to pick them up. None of them suspected that they might become ill, but then why would they?

To guarantee the plan's success, the homeowner had hired the right person. The mission had been accomplished without a hitch.

The homeowner was no longer making contact with the worker. The post office box had been cancelled. With the plan completed, the worker would never hear from the homeowner again.

###

Until Lee started working for the homeowner, he had never committed a crime. Thinking about it, he wondered if he had done something illegal. Exactly what had he done? Although he had his suspicions he really didn't know why C.J. Smith wanted the golf balls spread over the golf course.

Guilt was consuming Lee, not knowing what effect if any the golf balls would have on anyone handling them. For days, he pondered over whether he should call the police anonymously. What could he say without implicating himself?

Even with the guilt, Lee considered blackmailing C.J. Smith. The word sounded criminal, but why shouldn't he benefit from what he had done. Money would definitely help keep Lee's mouth shut. Lee had been used and why shouldn't he take advantage of the situation?

The problem with the blackmail was that Lee had no idea who C. J. Smith was. Unfortunately, Lee had made a mistake by using his real name and he knew C.J. Smith was not a real name. The only thing Lee was sure of was that C.J. Smith was a homeowner and probably lived on the golf course.

The post office box had been closed which meant all

communication was over. Every morning while Lee performed his duties, he searched for clues that might tell him who C.J. Smith was. The reality was that with the job done, he would probably never be contacted by the homeowner again.

The last thing Lee wanted was to be the one the police arrested. C.J. Smith held all the cards. Lee was vulnerable and it would be easy to point the finger at him if anything went wrong.

After all, was the substance he placed on the golf balls harmful? Only C.J. Smith knew for sure. Why didn't he ask these questions before now? He needed a plan to protect himself, but for now he would wait and watch.

CHAPTER 65

For weeks, the Marion County Police had made nightly rounds on the golf courses, but had nothing to show for their efforts. The police suspected that some of the homeowners had information, but for whatever reasons they were not cooperating.

The lack of cooperation had surprised and disappointed the police. They thought that residents of a retirement community would jump at the chance to help apprehend wrongdoers.

Lieutenant Wong was the officer-in-charge of the golf course investigations and did not want to continue wasting the county's money and time. He decided to take another course of action, hoping to produce results.

Tonight was different than the other nights. Woody had readied himself to go out onto the golf course, but something was nagging at him. The uneasiness was more than just nerves. He couldn't explain what was bothering him.

Stepping out of the lanai door, apprehension hit Woody like a strong gush of wind. When Woody learned that Lenny had been responsible for his head injury, he had lost his desire for seeking revenge on the golfers. He was no longer feeling the same level of satisfaction that initially drove him to this point.

Tonight, Woody's gut was saying, don't do it, but it wasn't enough to stop him. When Woody crossed the golf course, the surroundings seemed eerie.

Several times when he glanced over his shoulder he thought the shadows behind the trees were human. The image reminded him of children playing hide-and-seek. Instead of the quiet or typical sounds of Mother Nature, Woody could have sworn that the low tones he heard were more like people whispering.

The urge was for Woody to turn around and run, but something made him continue. Carefully, he walked, glancing around to see who or what was lurking on the golf course. The last of the screws were thrown and Woody began to breathe more easily. He had achieved what he had set out to do.

Woody had his hand on the lanai door when bright lights illuminated his back yard. He turned. "What the hell is going on?"

Cee and Les were sitting on the lanai talking when they noticed the shining lights off in the distance on the golf course. They grabbed their binoculars and looked.

"Cee, you're the one with the sixth sense. What do you think is going on?"

"Come on, Les. It doesn't take a mathematician to figure this out. The police are about to nab our mystery man—The Golf Course Menace is about to be caught."

CHAPTER 66

The lights were blinding. Woody blinked several times, trying to clear his vision so he could see. What was going on?

The Police Officer approached him. "Don't move. Put your hands in the air, above your head."

Woody closed his eyes and let out a heavy sigh. No one had to answer his question. He was about to face his biggest fear.

"Sir, turn around slowly and spread your legs." The officer ran his hand up and down Woody's body. When the procedure was complete, the officer said, "Woodward Roberts, you're under arrest."

The next words Woody heard as the cuffs were put on his hands were the familiar Miranda statement. "You have the right to remain silent. Anything you say can be used against you in a court of law...."

As the police officer continued to read Woody his rights, the words were drown out by his own thoughts of—*there is nothing sweet about revenge when you get caught.*

With all the formalities out of the way, Woody was placed in a police car. He was transported to the Marion County Police Station. Once inside the station, Woody's finger prints and picture were taken. Then, he was led to a small room and was told to sit in one of the chairs.

Before the Police Officer closed the door, he said, "Someone will be with you shortly."

Woody tried to remain calm. After all, he wasn't in a position to argue or make demands. Before the police officer left him, Woody said in a firm but gentle voice, "I'm entitled to make one phone call and I would like to make it now." As an afterthought, he added, "Please."

The officer brought a cordless phone to Woody. He punched in the numbers and waited.

"Why was he calling Justin Williams?" He knew why. Justin could be trusted, would not be judgmental, and he wouldn't ask a lot of unnecessary questions.

"Hello." Woody stopped holding his breath when he heard Justin's voice. "Justin, it's Woody."

Woody wanted to share more with Justin, but he couldn't. He was standing in the open with no privacy. Besides, the call was probably being recorded.

The strain in Woody's voice told Justin that something was wrong. He cut straight to the point. "What's up?"

Woody took a deep breath. "I apologize for calling so late." His voice cracked. He murmured, "I've been arrested."

Justin wanted to ask Woody why he had been arrested, but this wasn't the time or the place. Instead, he said the words Woody wanted to hear. "I'll be right there, but I need to know where you are?"

"I'm at the Marion County Police Station."

"Okay, I'll be there as soon as I can."

Justin was curious as to why Woody had called him instead of Amanda, but again he did not ask. While Justin was driving to the station, he called her. "Hi, Amanda. This is Justin."

"I don't know how to tell you this, but Woody has been arrested. He's at the Marion County Police Station."

She screamed in a loud, high-pitched voice. "Arrested! I can't believe this is happening."

With a slight pause, Justin said, "Amanda, I'm really sorry I had to be the one to tell you."

When Amanda spoke again, her voice was back to her normal pitch. "Justin, I'm the one who should be apologizing. You're the messenger and I took it out on you. I should be grateful that Woody had a friend he could call."

Through gritted teeth she added. "After all he didn't see fit to call me. Do you know why he was arrested?"

"I'm sorry, but he didn't say. To be honest, I didn't ask. I'm on my way to the Police Station, now."

"Thanks Justin. I'll meet you there."

Before Justin hung up Amanda said firmly. "When you see Woody, please tell him not to say anything. Tell him not to answer any questions."

CHAPTER 67

After Woody made his one call the police officer took the phone and left him. He sat down in the hard, steel chair.

Woody glanced at his surroundings. The walls as well as the steel table and chairs were in various shades of gray. The room's coloring was a reflection of his mood, depressing. The lighting was provided by a single bulb hanging from the ceiling.

Nothing was hung on the walls to make the room welcoming. A glass mirror covered most of the far wall. Again, Woody found humor in the police. Everyone knew that anyone standing outside the mirror could see inside and was privy to everything taking place in the room.

Being married to a lawyer Woody was familiar with the system and what was going to happen. Closing his eyes, he placed his head on the table.

A loud bang made Woody jump. Two officers walked in and Woody straightened himself up in the chair.

"Mr. Roberts. Hello." The officer made introductions.

Woody recognized Lieutenant Wong. He was the officer who had been on the golf course. The other police officer, Jefferson Martin, he had never seen before.

"Is everything okay? Would you like something to drink?"

To the first question, Woody nodded and declined the drink offer. Another police trick, fill the suspect up with fluids and then the person will do and say anything just to use the restroom.

Officer Wong sat across from Woody while Officer Martin stood. Wong took a notepad from his inside coat pocket. He smiled.

"Mr. Roberts, I would like to ask you some questions?"

Woody chewed the inside of his mouth. As much as he wanted to cooperate he knew better than to answer questions without a lawyer.

"Mr. Roberts, did you hear what I said, I would like to ask you a few questions."

"Uh…I'm sorry, but without a lawyer I'm not answering any questions."

CHAPTER 68

Arriving at the Police Station, Justin walked up to the officer sitting at the desk near the door. "Excuse me, but I'm here to see Woody... Woodward Roberts."

The police flipped through several papers on his desk. "Please have a seat sir. Someone will be with you."

As instructed, Justin took a seat. He prayed Woody was not answering any questions. Justin was reading his Bible when Amanda arrived.

Amanda rushed over to Justin. From her exterior, she appeared calm. They greeted each other.

"Have you seen Woody?"

"No. When I inquired about him I was told to have a seat."

Amanda turned around and left Justin standing. She walked over to the officer.

"Where's Mr. Woodward Roberts?"

"Ma'am, he's with a police officer."

"I'm his lawyer." With authority Amanda said, "Now, go get whoever is in charge and let them know that Mr. Roberts' lawyer is here."

The officer rose from his chair and left Amanda standing at the desk as he strolled down the corridor. She turned and walked over to where Justin was standing.

"I need to see Woody. Justin, thanks for everything. It's late and if you need to leave, I understand."

The offer was tempting. "I'll wait in case you need something. Is there anything I can do or anyone you want me to call?"

"No and Justin I really appreciate everything you've done."

The officer walked over to Amanda. "Excuse me ma'am. Please follow me."

Amanda was led to a small room. When the door opened, Woody was sitting at the table. When she walked into the room, Woody lowered his head. He didn't acknowledge her until she sat down at the table.

The silence Amanda brought into the room made the temperature feel as if they were in a freezer. Amanda laid a tablet on the table. She was professional, treating Woody like he was one of her clients.

Nervously, she tapped the table with the end of her long manicured fingernails. She was fighting to keep her emotions under control.

Woody reached across the table, wanting to touch his wife, but she pulled away from him. After what seemed like hours, Woody cleared his throat. His voice strained as he began to speak.

"I'm sorry Mandy…Amanda. I'm really sorry."

"Not as sorry as I am." Amanda's voice was full of disgust. "Woody what did you do to get arrested? What are you being charged with?"

He shrugged. "I wasn't told why I was arrested. When I arrived the police asked if I would answer a few questions."

"Did you answer any questions?"

Woody was hurt by her tone and that she had asked him that. "No. I knew better than that."

Amanda didn't miss Woody's wounded expression. Woody may not understand, but being arrested is serious.

"Good! Were you read your rights?"

Woody didn't answer right away. He felt their conversation was more like lawyer and client than husband and wife. Not once did she ask how he was doing. He wanted Mandy, his wife.

"Yes, an officer read me the Miranda Act."

"That's good. Then what happened?"

Amanda wanted details. She would comfort Woody later. At the moment, she had other concerns to worry about. She knew the legal system far better than Woody and it was important to understand the seriousness of what he was being charged with.

"Well I was…"

"Wait, before you say anything else, please tell me what you were doing at the time of the arrest?"

This was a question Woody dreaded answering. If at all possible, he would prefer to wait until they were in the confines of their home. What he needed was a hot shower to clear his head and to talk in a friendlier environment. Amanda had crossed her arms across her chest and glared at him, waiting for him to answer.

Woody's initial words came out in a stutter. "I...I...was....was at home when the police arrested me."

Amanda dropped her arms and leaned on the table, her voice hissing. "You were arrested at home. What were you doing?"

Woody didn't meet Amanda's eyes. "I was standing at the lanai door when the police approached me."

Amanda covered her mouth to stifle a loud outburst. Her voice was firm, but when her words were uttered they sounded more like a growl. "Tell me, you're not the Golf Course Menace! Woody, answer me!"

Their eyes met. Woody didn't have to answer. She knew from his expression that he was guilty.

So many things ran through Amanda's head until she could no longer hold back her emotions. The anger from her voice blasted him. "Woody, of all the dumb, childish things you have done. Have you lost your mind? You put your health at risk for what, revenge?"

Amanda waited, wanting an explanation. Her eyes narrowed, boring into him as if she was pounding a nail into wood.

Once or twice Woody opened his mouth to speak, but the words never came forth. Yes, his actions might have seemed juvenile, but someone had to protect his property. She could never understand. That's why he didn't share his plan with her because he knew she would never have approved.

Amanda expected Woody to say something in his defense, but he sat staring at his folded hands. She stood up to leave. This was a waste of time and their conversation was going nowhere. Woody wasn't going to give her any answers until he was ready and then only on his terms.

CHAPTER 69

Amanda approached the officer-in-charge. Although she didn't know the man personally she had seen him around the courthouse. A familiar face was nice to see, even if it wasn't necessarily friendly considering the circumstances.

"Hi, Mrs. Roberts."

Amanda wished she could recall the officer's name, but before she could, he offered his hand and said, "I'm Lieutenant Wong." She returned the handshake, happy that he had said his name.

Officer Wong smothered a chuckle. "I understand your husband has been up to some mischief."

Amanda shook her head. "Do men ever grow up?" She didn't wait for a response to her question. "What is he being charged with?"

"He's being charged with criminal mischief."

"Thank God," escaped from Amanda's mouth. She hoped she didn't show too much joy, but she was elated. She had worried that he was being charged with trespassing and vandalism which would carry possible jail time, a hefty fine, or both.

We believe he's the one responsible for the golf cart flat tires." Officer Wong said, "You can take him home."

Amanda's eyes were wide with surprise. "What about bail?"

"Since you're an officer of the court, we'll release him to you. However, first thing in the morning at nine o'clock, he has to appear in court. You know the drill."

"Thanks." Amanda shook the officer's hand. "Thanks for everything."

When Amanda returned to the room, Woody had laid his head down on the table. Seeing him, Amanda wanted to run to him, to make sure he wasn't sick, especially since he did not look up when she entered the room.

"Woody! Woody!"

Slowly, he raised his head.

"Are you okay?"

His voice was hoarse, his eyes red with dark circles underneath them. His face had fatigue or maybe it was worry written all over it. She wanted to be supportive, but considering his childish prank, she wasn't about to console him.

Rather than sit, Amanda stood, annoyance seeping through her voice. "You're being released until the morning. You should be grateful that you won't have to spend the night in jail."

Woody was sure that Mandy, being an officer of the court was the reason he was being released. No matter why, he was free and could go home. He jumped up and hugged Mandy tight.

Amanda was limp in Woody's embrace. She pulled away.

In a low murmur, Woody asked, "Did you find out what I was being charged with?"

"Yes, you're being charged with criminal mischief. In the morning, you must appear in court."

CHAPTER 70

Once home, Amanda did not waste time making telephone calls. She had to find Woody a lawyer. Working for the DA's office, she could not represent him. Besides, she believed that it was never a good idea for a wife to represent her husband and vice versa.

Woody watched and listened as Mandy placed each call. The third call grabbed his attention. Unlike the other calls, Mandy's voice was friendlier and more casual. In addition, there was a tad too much familiarity in the conversation. Under different circumstances he would have questioned her about the person. Instead, he filed the name in his memory bank for future reference.

Mandy hung up the phone, smiled and let out a sigh. "Finally, I got someone to represent you. I hope you realize that it wasn't easy."

Instead of Woody thanking his wife for all her efforts, he let his distrust take over. "How well do you know this lawyer?"

Amanda knew where this conversation was headed and she was too tired to engage in a question and answer session about her relationship with the lawyer she had retained.

Perhaps she was partly the blame for his jealousy, but for once he should let it go. Had he not been listening to how many calls she had made? Does he not understand the severity of what he had done and how badly this could turn out?

Shaking her head, she finally answered. "Yes, I know Riley Lewis well. We met in law school. You couldn't do any better when it comes to a criminal defense lawyer."

"Wait a minute. If the charge is minimal then why do I need a good criminal lawyer?" Under his breath he muttered. "I don't mind spending money, but this seems like a waste."

Amanda did not mince her words. "Woody, listen to me. Sometimes, things go wrong in court. Why do you think innocent people end up in jail even though they had a lawyer?" She didn't wait for Woody to answer. "You get what you pay for!"

With her hand on her hip and pointing a finger at him, she warned. "You had better listen to me and follow the advice of the lawyer I just hired or you could end up behind bars. Do you understand me?"

Woody hung his head. He knew he should be grateful for everything she had done. To be truthful, this was more personal than anything. He kept thinking about the man she had hired. Who was he? Did they have a sexual relationship?

Jealousy was a demon Woody had difficulty controlling. When he heard Amanda laughing and chatting with her buddy, he couldn't stop thinking about what they might have meant to each other. It doesn't matter that it happened before they married. The point is she would see him again and be reminded of what they once had.

Sleep for Woody did not come easy. All he could think about was the discussion, no, it was more like an argument he and Amanda had before they went to bed.

Despite the advice Amanda had given him earlier, Woody was unrelenting. "I did nothing wrong. I want to plead innocent." He defended his actions and believed they were warranted.

Amanda listened and warned, "Woody, under no circumstances will you plead innocent. The police caught you in the act."

Quickly, their discussion turned into an argument that had lasted late into the night. The last words Amanda said before she turned her back to Woody were, "Do whatever you want, but remember, you did the crime and therefore you could do time."

In the morning, Woody looked in the mirror. The lack of sleep was visible by the deep dark circles and puffy eyes. Looking close, he could see every tiny line around his eyes, mouth, and forehead. The words—old and haggard—described the reflection in the mirror.

Looking through Amanda's make-up, Woody considered

using the liquid she sometimes used to hide her under eye flaws. As quickly as he had thought about it, he decided against it. He wondered when he had become so vain.

While Woody finished dressing, he smelled the coffee aroma in the air which meant Amanda was already up. When Woody joined her in the kitchen she had breakfast on the table.

"Good morning." One glance at Woody and she felt guilty and responsible for him not getting much sleep, but neither had she. Most of the night, Woody had tossed and turned.

Cheerfully, she said, "I'm glad you wore your navy blue, double-breasted suit. Not many men can wear an off- the-rack suit and look as good as you do in it."

Any other time Woody would have appreciated her praises. He forced a smile. His response to Amanda's greeting and compliment was a mumble. The sight of the food made Woody's stomach queasy. Usually, he required a hardy breakfast to start the day, but this morning he didn't dare eat, afraid that if he ate, it would come back up.

Amanda poured Woody a cup of coffee. "You're not going to eat anything?"

"I'm not hungry." He didn't bother to tell her why he didn't want to eat.

"Woody, please eat something. Court hearings don't always run on time." Amanda urged. "At least have a slice of toast."

Woody growled, "Fine, but make it dry."

Since Woody was in such a bad mood, Amanda left him alone with his thoughts. She finished dressing and returned to see that he had not touched the toast.

Amanda touched his shoulder. "Are you ready?"

"Not really, but what choice do I have?"

Worried lines crossed Amanda's forehead. She smiled, but her voice was firm. "Woody, if you listen to your lawyer everything will work out just fine."

He sighed making a comment under his breath. "That's easy for you to say."

CHAPTER 71

Driving to the courthouse, Amanda turned on the radio. In a huff, Woody reached over and turned the radio station off.

"The last thing I want to hear is news about murders, robberies, and kidnappings. And most of all, I don't want to hear a story about my arrest."

"I'm sorry. I thought the radio would be a distraction and would help take your mind off your problems."

Woody grumbled. "Well, maybe if you had turned on a music station."

The rest of the ride was tense. Despite the car's air conditioning blowing cool air the inside temperature felt hot and stuffy.

By the time they arrived at the courthouse, Woody's underarms were wet. He thought, *"Yeah, don't let them see you sweat."*

His only consolation was that he was wearing a dark navy blue suit that would hide any signs of perspiration. When Mandy and Woody entered the courthouse, she stopped a young man.

"Woody, I'll be with you in a minute. Please wait over there for me."

Woody stood nearby and watched the two of them. The conversation between the two of them was brief.

Mandy joined Woody and they proceeded down the hall. "I've got good news. The judge hearing your case is fair and more lenient than most."

If Mandy's remark was intended to be encouraging and comforting, it wasn't. In fact, the comment made Woody's stomach churn. Taking a handkerchief from his pocket, he wiped the stream of sweat from his forehead and the sides of his face.

Woody was anxious about meeting his lawyer. He was kicking himself for not talking to Riley Lewis. Instead, he had allowed Mandy to handle everything. When he stated that it would have been nice to have met Riley before the court hearing, Mandy's response was less than comforting. He recalled her words.

"Woody, what is the problem? We'll meet Riley before the hearing. We've agreed to meet early. That way, you'll get the opportunity to talk. Everything will be fine."

Mandy might be used to court proceedings but he was not. Her tone was making him feel as if she couldn't understand why he was so concerned. According to her everything would be fine, but would it?

Approaching the courtroom, he became more uneasy when Riley was not there. Again, Mandy dismissed his concerns.

With less than twenty minutes before Woody's court appearance, his lawyer had not shown up. Amanda had busied herself with her Blackberry. Woody was pacing.

Amanda glanced up. "Why don't you have a seat? Riley will be...." Mandy stood up. "There she is now."

Woody smiled as he watched a woman approaching them, hurriedly. He was relieved that the lawyer Mandy was so fond of had turned out to be a woman. Unless...Woody's mind was racing, but soon dismissed the thought. Mandy would never have a love interest in a woman.

"Good morning, Riley. How are you?"

"Hey, Amanda." They hugged. "It's good to see you. I apologize for my lateness, but I had an emergency."

Riley turned to Woody and extended her hand. They shook. "You must be Woodward."

"Please call me Woody."

"Let's sit over here so we can discuss your case." Riley repeated almost everything Amanda had told him. He liked Riley and felt confident about facing the judge.

Everything went as Mandy and Riley had predicted. In fact, the judge was more understanding about Woody's actions than expected. He would have to pay for all the golf cart damages, perform 90 hours of community service, and pay a fine. The best news was that Woody would have no jail or probation time.

The reason for the leniency was because the judge once lived on a golf course and understood Woody's plight all too well. He did give him a strong warning. "I know how beautiful a golf course view can be, but you might want to consider moving."

CHAPTER 69

As Les and Cee sat on the lanai eating breakfast, Les picked up the morning newspaper. One of the front page headlines caught his attention. "Cee, listen to this. The Golf Course Menace was arrested."

"What? When, how, who was it?"

"As usual, you were right about why the police were on the golf course."

Cee sighed. "Les, if you think about it. There was no other reason for the police, the bright lights and all the activity that was taking place on the golf course."

"That may be true, but there might have been something else going on. You never know."

Cee exhaled loudly. "It doesn't matter now. Just tell me what the article says? I want to know who was arrested."

"I haven't read the article." Les skimmed over the details. "You're not going to believe this. The person responsible was none other than our neighbor, Woodward Roberts."

"Oh, my God!" Cee stopped, shaking her head. "You never know about people. I guess we shouldn't be surprised. I mean if I had been hit in the head by a stray golf ball and the guilty party was never caught I would probably seek revenge in some way."

"I hear you, but…."

"Please, Les. Regardless of what you may think, I like what Mr. Roberts did. He took care of business."

"Let's not give the guy a gold medal. He could have hurt someone."

"Come on, Les. A few golf carts were damaged. So what? Did he kill anyone?"

"That's not the point. You can't go around taking matters into your own hands and believe that there are no consequences even when you have good intentions."

Cee wasn't listening to Les as she rattled on. "You never know about your neighbors. I mean people expect me to be nosy and even a little cunning because that's who I am, but Mr. Roberts. He seemed too cool and laid back to be the vindictive type."

"Well, that's not the impression I got when we visited him in the hospital. I thought he might have a slight temper and was capable of settling the score with someone who had wronged him."

"What else does the article say?"

"Let me see. That's about it. With his arrest, the article states that golfers can rest easy."

Cee murmured, "I think the golfers better still watch their backs."

"What makes you say that?"

Cee didn't answer him. "By any chance was there any mention in the paper about the golfers who have been going to the hospital in droves?"

Les was taken back. "Why did you say the people with the unexplained disease were golfers?"

"I might be wrong, but I might know what's making these people sick."

Les put the newspaper down and turned his full attention to Cee. "Exactly what do you know that the doctors haven't been able to figure out?"

"Why do I have to continue to remind you that I have a sixth sense about these things? Remember when we lived in the villas and I helped with the arrest of those robbers?"

"I do, but explain to me what you think you know about the unexplained disease."

"You might think I'm crazy or off base, but I think the people in the hospital might have been poisoned."

"How did you come to that conclusion? I mean do you have any conclusive evidence?"

"Oh, listen to my husband. You sound like the police."

"That's not it Cee. I don't want you going around making those types of accusations without proof. I think you should think about what you're saying and take it slow."

Cee exploded. "I can't do that. People are at risk and someone could die. I don't think you have to be a genius to think like the police or a criminal. For weeks, I've been studying the facts. First of all, everyone in the hospital is a golfer."

Les was firm. "You don't know that.'

"Okay, but humor me. Another common factor, they all golfed in The Villages."

Les shook his head. "That's another fact you can't substantiate."

"Yes and no. Shirley, you know from the hospital's volunteer staff, has been feeding me information about all the patients who have been admitted with this virus or whatever they're calling it."

Cee watched Les opening his mouth, but before he could interrupt her she continued. "Based on that information I've been coming up with my own deductions. And…" Cee's voice drifted off.

"What else?" Instead of Cee answering Les, she stood up and went into the house. When she returned she had one of the pay-to-go phones in her hand. Les watched as she punched in a telephone number.

"Who are you calling?"

CHAPTER 72

Cee put her hand over the phone's mouth piece and whispered, "I'm calling the police."

Les rolled his eyes. He loved his wife, but he wasn't following Cee's process of elimination. He wanted to stop her, but instead he sat quietly, watching and waiting to see what she was going to say to the police.

Cee was pacing and did not sit down until she started talking. "Hello."

A low baritone voice responded. "This is the Police Department, how may I help you?"

"This is ..." Cee stopped. She almost made a mistake. She had no intention of giving her name. She went straight to the reason for the call.

"I have information that may help solve the mystery regarding the sick people in the hospital."

"Ma'am, why are you calling the police?"

"Because I believe a crime has been committed."

"And, what crime would that be?"

"Well, I read in the paper that the Golf Course Menace has been caught."

The officer sighed. Daily, they received far too many helpful calls from people who believe they had information that could help solve crimes.

In a soft but, firm voice, the officer said, "Ma'am, I don't want to be rude or to hurry you along, but as you stated the Golf Course Menace has been apprehended."

Indignantly, Cee replied, "I started off by saying that. What I want to say is that I believe there is a connection between the Golf Course Menace and the people that are sick in the hospital."

Cee paused, thinking the officer might have something to say, but when he didn't she continued, "I believe the Golf Course Menace was not only responsible for the golf cart damages, but he might have also poisoned the golfers."

"Ma'am, I'm not following what you're implying."

Frustration was the only word to describe Cee's attitude. Continuing the conversation with this officer was useless. She hung up and looked at Les. "Don't say it."

Cee wasn't discouraged and redialed the Sheriff Department and asked to speak to Lieutenant Wong. To her surprise she was actually connected to him.

"Hello, this is Lieutenant Wong. How may I help you?"

Rather than use a nice and friendly approach, Cee went straight to the point. "Sir, I have information that might help solve the mystery involving the unexplained disease that is affecting so many people."

"Ma'am, before you go any further, I need to obtain some information from you. First, may I have your name?"

Cee started shaking her head. No way was she giving her name. Besides, she didn't want to stay on the line too long. She might be using a pay-to-go phone, but with today's technology, the police may still be able to trace the call.

"Ma'am. Ma'am. Are you still there?"

"I am, but my name isn't important. The police need to question the Golf Course Menace." Cee changed her tactic. "If you want to help all those sick people in the hospital, the doctors might want to test the patients for poisoning."

Since the woman would not give her name, Wong knew he didn't have much time before she would hang up. "What type of poison?"

"I don't know. Maybe he used a chemical or fertilizer that would blend in with whatever The Villages spread over the golf courses." With that comment, the phone went dead.

CHAPTER 73

Lieutenant Wong sat, mulling over the telephone call. During a high profile case, it wasn't unusual to receive prank calls and an array of anonymous tips, especially when a reward is posted. However, this was different, there was no ongoing investigation regarding the hospital and its sick patients.

The call might result in being nothing but a prank, but with so many people, including his mother being sick, he had to follow-up. Lieutenant Wong gave the call lots of consideration before mentioning it to his friend and co-worker, Jefferson Martin.

Wong provided Martin with the details. "The caller was a woman, with a hint of a southern accent. Her voice didn't sound young, but yet she didn't seem old. There was something in her tone that made the call seem truthful."

He rubbed his hand over his face. "Anyway, she believes the people in the hospital and the Golf Course Menace are somehow connected. She thinks poison might be the reason why the people are sick."

"Great, but what is she basing her facts on?"

Wong shrugged. "I don't know." He ran his fingers through his hair. "She was reluctant to give me her name. Instead, she emphasized the need for the police to investigate what she was saying and most of all the Golf Course Menace needed to be questioned."

"I'm confused, why did this woman call the police?"

"She believes that it is our responsibility to protect people from being killed. She reminded me that if someone dies, it will be our responsibility."

"Is that what's bugging you?"

Wong shook his head. "I don't know. I guess the woman caught my attention because of my mom. She has that virus and the hospital seems to be clueless as to what's causing it and how to treat it. In the meantime, my mom doesn't seem to be getting better and more and more people keep getting sick."

Martin wasn't sure he wanted to ask but he did. "Has anyone died?"

"Not yet. Maybe that's why I want to follow-up on this tip."

CHAPTER 74

When Wong and Martin arrived at the hospital they walked up to the information desk where a gray haired male volunteer greeted them.

Wong showed the man his badge. "I'm Lieutenant Wong and this is Officer Martin. We hope you can help us."

The man grinned. "That's what I'm here for. Now, what would you like to know?"

"Uh…we're here regarding the people with the unexplained disease. We would like to talk to the doctor or doctors in charge of those individuals."

Without hesitation, the man provided them with the information. "There are two doctors assigned to the case and they are Dr. Olivia Herman and Dr. Wayne Dean."

The volunteer stopped and looked at a chart. "According to the schedule, both doctors are conducting rounds. Go to the third floor. That's where you'll find both doctors. Is there anything else I can do for you?"

In unison, Wong and Martin said no and thanked the man. They took the elevator and when they reached the floor, Martin was stunned.

"My God, I had no idea."

"The first time I came to visit my mom I had the same reaction. Everyone sick is being isolated to this floor."

They approached the nurse's station. Wong took the lead. "Hi." He flashed his badge. "We're looking for Dr. Herman."

Before Wong continued, the nurse stated, "She's in with a patient. If you wait here she should be finished shortly."

"Can you page her?" asked Martin.

The nurse chewed her lower lip and reluctantly picked up the phone. As she spoke, the loud speaker blared, "Paging Dr. Herman, paging Dr. Herman."

Putting the phone back in its cradle, the nurse peered at both men. Although the woman said nothing, it was easy to read her body language. "There, I've paged her."

"Thank you, miss. They walked away from the desk. Martin said to Wong. "I'm going to the Men's Room."

"While you do that, I'm going to check in on my mom. It won't take but a minute. "

Martin had taken a seat and was glancing through a magazine when Wong returned. Martin glanced up. "How's your mom?"

"Thanks for asking, but there hasn't been much change. I'm thankful considering her other health problems." Wong didn't want to discuss his mom. "I guess Dr. Herman hasn't responded to the page yet."

Wong motioned to Martin. When they approached the nurse, they didn't have to ask as she pointed. "There's Dr. Herman."

The doctor's legs were long and slender. Her steps were slow and deliberate as she strolled down the corridor. When she reached the nurse's stations she said, "I'm sorry it took so long to respond to the page, but I was in the middle of examining a patient. What's up?"

The nurse tilted her head. "These men are police officers and they have been waiting for you."

Dr. Herman turned to Wong and Martin, greeting them with a handshake, apologizing for causing them any inconvenience. They nodded, indicating that they understood. They both flashed their badges as Wong introduced himself and Martin.

"How might I help you?"

Wong noticed the nurse at the desk listening to their conversation even though she busied herself, picking up and flipping through files. "Let's step over here, if you don't mind."

When they were out of the nurses' range of hearing, Wong continued in a lowered voice. "I received an anonymous tip regarding the unexplained disease and we're following up on it." He paused. "The person who called indicated that the patients might have been poisoned."

Dr. Herman's eyes widened and whispered, "Poisoned."

Martin asked, "Were the patients tested for poisons?"

The doctor bit her lower lip. Even though the CDC had been

contacted, Dr. Herman didn't recall all the tests the patients had been given. Their focus had been on a new strain of virus or flu.

"I'm not sure. Let's go to my office and I'll verify what tests were conducted."

Inside Dr. Herman's office, she offered both men a chair, across from her desk. Wong and Martin sat down. Quietly, they watched Dr. Herman as she picked up two large file folders that were on top of a pile of papers. She placed the two folders in front of her. She opened up the first one and used her finger to skim over the first page and did the same as she turned to the next page. When she finished with the first folder, she set it aside and picked up the second one.

Setting those folders aside, Dr. Herman picked up a binder. She closed the notebook and stated with certainty. "I did a quick review of information regarding my patients and those of Dr. Dean's. All of the patients were only tested for food poisoning and those tests came back negative."

Wong was direct. "Is there any reason why the patients weren't tested for poisoning?"

Dr. Herman guarded her response. "You have to understand the hospital was inundated with large numbers of people that had flu-like symptoms." She shrugged. "We did what we thought was best and treated them accordingly."

Martin was curious. "Then why was the CDC notified?"

"Standard procedure dictates that CDC be called when a sizable number of people are being treated for similar symptoms without an explanation of its origin."

The room was silent. Wong pulled a notepad from his suit pocket and was taking notes. Without looking up, he asked, "Is the hospital or the CDC conducting any type of analysis, searching for a commonality among the sick?"

"Like what?"

"You know, do these patients have anything in common?"

Dr. Herman folded her hands in a tent leaned forward and shared. "We tried and came up with nothing. That's what's making this so mysterious." This time Dr. Herman asked a question. "Did the caller say why the individuals might have been poisoned?"

Martin sighed. "The police department receives lots of tips. In this particular case, the caller, a woman, hung up before I could ask any detailed questions."

Dr. Herman was confused. "But yet, you're following up on the tip. May I ask why?"

Martin was honest with his response. "It's nothing but a gut feeling." He continued, "Based on what we've shared, will you test the patients for poisoning?"

"Yes, right away. I'll also talk to Dr. Dean about testing his patients as well. You might want to talk to Dr. Dean, but we consult daily on all the patients and I can assure you he doesn't know any more than I've told you."

CHAPTER 75

When Wong and Martin left the hospital, Wong insisted on paying a visit to Woodward Roberts. Martin wasn't in agreement with Wong's decision.

The procedure was to call ahead and schedule an appointment to follow-up on a lead. Instead, they were making an unannounced visit because Wong had a strong feeling about the tip.

He blasted Wong. "Come on, man. You need to rethink what we're about to do. I don't think we've done enough footwork on this. The only evidence we have tying Roberts to a possible crime is your gut feeling and the anonymous tip."

Wong was annoyed. "Chill out man. Quit worrying about nothing. This isn't the first time I've followed a lead, with little or no information. In the past when I've followed my instincts what has been the results? Wong didn't wait for Martin to reply. "Every time, I was right on the money. So quit your whining."

Martin wanted to argue the point. This was totally different and Wong knew it. They were dealing with a D.A.'s spouse and everyone knew Amanda Roberts was a person who did everything by the book and she was someone you didn't mess with. Why put their careers on the line because of a hunch? If they were wrong, they could end up being demoted or worse, fired.

On their drive to the Roberts' home, Martin tried one more time. "Amanda Roberts is not going to appreciate us making an unannounced house call to question her husband."

Wong responded with venom. "So what if Amanda Roberts works in the D.A.'s office? As far as her husband is concerned, we're merely gathering information. Besides, with his recent arrest, I'm sure he is still retaining a lawyer. If that's the case, he won't talk to us anyway."

Martin glanced at Wong. "I hear you, man, but I don't like it. I want to go on record stating that I didn't want to make this visit."

"Are you saying you don't have my back?"

"That's not what I'm saying, Wong. As a cop, if this was your family member, you would want...no, you would expect a heads up."

Wong ignored the comment as he pulled into the Roberts' driveway. When they climbed out of the car and approached the house, Martin rang the doorbell.

Woody had been waiting for a delivery. When the door bell rang, he peeped out the window. It was Wong and Martin. He was curious about why they were paying him a visit.

Rather than speculate and worry about what they wanted, Woody had an idea. Before answering the door, he grabbed the cordless phone and dialed Mandy's number. She picked up on the second ring.

"Hi, dear. What a pleasant surprise. What's up?"

"I'm about to answer the door and I want you to listen."

"Woody...Woody." Amanda had the notion to hang up. She couldn't imagine what was going on. She shook her head. Woody was always up to something, no different than a young, mischievous child.

Again, the doorbell rang. Before opening the door, Woody placed the phone behind his back. "Hello Lieutenant Wong. What brings you here today?"

"Hello Mr. Roberts." He motioned to the other man. "You remember Officer Jefferson Martin."

Woody nodded his head. He didn't bother to shake either man's hand. "How may I help you gentlemen?"

Martin took the lead. "We would prefer to come in and explain everything to you."

Amanda yelled, "Woody, Woody. Pick up, Woody.

The sound of Mandy's voice caused all three men to look at each other. Woody brought his arm forward, producing the phone. He held it forward.

"Gentlemen, my wife, Amanda Roberts, the D.A. is on the phone."

Woody put the phone to his ear. "Did you hear that?"

"Yes, Woody and don't answer any questions without Riley being present."

An awkward moment filled the space that separated Woody, Wong, and Martin. Woody eyeing each man before he repeated what Mandy had told him.

"On the advice of my wife, I will not be answering any questions without my lawyer present."

Wong cleared his throat. "Fine, Mr. Roberts. Do you think you and your lawyer can report to the Marion Police Station, tomorrow, say around 10:00 am?"

Woody didn't commit. "Do you have a business card?"

Martin reached inside his coat pocket and withdrew a card and handed it to him.

"I'll contact my lawyer and Ms. Lewis will notify you as to whether tomorrow and the time are convenient for us to meet with you."

CHAPTER 76

Over the weekend, Dr. Herman had not received one emergency call regarding the sick patients. She was relieved especially about the one critically ill man, Bradshaw Witherspoon.

Unlike the other patients, Mr. Witherspoon had not remained stable. The last time Dr. Herman examined him, his condition seemed to be worsening.

She wished the poisoning test results had been completed. The CDC was working hard and she knew it was a top priority, but the waiting was difficult knowing that so many people could be at risk.

Monday morning, Dr. Herman stopped at the nurse's station. She picked up several charts and scanned them. The first person on her rounds was Mr. Witherspoon. While flipping through his chart, the machines hooked up to him began beeping.

Dr. Herman dropped the charts, ran to Mr. Witherspoon's bedside. She yelled, "Code Blue." He was flat lining.

Within seconds, a crash cart bolted through the door followed by doctors and nurses. Dr. Herman did everything she could to revive Mr. Witherspoon. In an exhausted tone, she uttered, "The time of death is 10:15 a.m.

Within the hour, the news had spread like a bad weed taking over a flower bed. The message was the same, "The man with the virus and was in critical condition, died." The whispers were filled with concern and sadness.

The outward response of the staff was guarded. Regardless of their feelings, they conducted their daily duties in a professional manner, especially when treating the sick patients. However, when the staff was alone most of them shared the same sentiments. One patient had died and they were concerned as to how many more might follow.

The sick individuals had been placed in four categories: sick, mildly sick, stable, and critical condition. Despite the hospital news releases neither the doctors nor the CDC were any closer to finding out what was making these people sick. Everyone knew the autopsy would provide answers, but again it would take time and that was something they didn't have.

Along with the man's death, information circulated quickly about the police meeting with Dr. Herman. That sparked a flood of rumors as to why the police were asking questions about the sick patients. Most of the buzz talked about the disease possibly being the work of terrorists to a possible government experiment.

Panic was beginning to fill the hospital corridors.

CHAPTER 77

The hospital was unable to keep the information from the public. Newspaper reporters, relatives of the sick patients, healthy and people with chronic illnesses flooded the hospital phone lines. Everyone demanded answers.

Detectives Wong and Martin heard about the man's death just before Woodward Roberts and his lawyer arrived. Officer Wong greeted both of them and showed them to a conference room.

Once everyone was seated, Martin asked the first question. "Mr. Roberts, you were recently arrested and pleaded guilty regarding the golf course incidents. Is that correct?"

Rather than respond, Woody nodded his head.

"Are you aware that hundreds of people have been admitted to the hospital due to some mysterious illness?"

Woody's lawyer, Riley Lewis, asked, "What does this have to do with my client?"

"Mr. Roberts, your revenge plot might have done more than damage flat tires. In fact, it might have turned deadly."

Woody flared, "What are you talking about? Why don't you quit chasing me around the tree and tell me what it is I'm supposed to have done?" Riley placed her hand on Woody's arm to silence him.

Wong asked the next question. "Mr. Roberts, why don't you tell us?"

"Tell you what?" He hunched his shoulders. "All I did was spread nails and screws on the golf course." Woody flew his hand up in the air. "That is all I did."

"Are you sure, Mr. Roberts? By any chance did you put anything else on the golf course?" Martin asked.

Woody was confused as he glanced at Riley. He shrugged, "I have no idea what you're talking about."

Wong and Martin took turns asking questions. They were relentless.

Wong said, "Everyone understands your motive for seeking

revenge, but what you didn't count on was people getting sick."

"Would you please stop saying that?" Woody was losing his temper. To calm himself, he inhaled and exhaled.

Speaking slowly, he tried to explain. "I used nails and screws to cause flat tires, nothing else." Woody looked at Riley. "Can we leave now?"

Before Riley could respond to Woody, Martin asked, "Are you saying you only used nails and screws and nothing else?"

"Well… I did use some golf balls to illuminate the golf course." Woody answered before Riley could stop him. She stood up.

"Gentlemen, this conversation is over unless you're placing my client under arrest."

CHAPTER 78

Cee had no idea whether the police followed up on her last call, but she prayed they had. In the past several days she had been trying to come up with other ways she could get the police to pay attention to her suggestion that poison might be the cause for people being sick. She had come up with nothing.

While Cee cooked breakfast, Les was reading the morning newspaper. He was skimming over the front page articles and was about to turn the page when he stopped. "Oh, my God."

"What's wrong, Les?"

"A man who had been sick in the hospital from the mysterious virus, died." Rapidly, he read the entire article.

"You're not going to believe this, but the police are actually investigating the death as being suspicious."

Cee's hand flew to her mouth as she plopped down in the nearby chair. "I knew it. I knew it. I'm sorry about the death, but now maybe the police will pay attention."

"One thing for sure, with the death occurring at the hospital, an autopsy will be conducted as a matter of routine procedure." Les paused. "Wait a minute. The man who died was Bradshaw Witherspoon."

Cee cocked her head to the side. "You mean our neighbor? That's the couple that's always cruising. But, I thought they were on a cruise."

"I think they were, but that was several weeks ago. When I golfed last week, I spoke to him."

Cee wanted to get back to the police investigation. "I guess the article didn't say anything about the police investigating the death."

"No. It's too soon for the police to release any information about the death being a murder. It just said that the death was ruled as suspicious."

Cee clapped her hands. "I bet the police are trying to set a trap by holding back specific details."

She nodded her head. "Yep, I bet that's exactly what they're doing." Then she added, "If only someone would have taken me more serious sooner."

Closely, Les watched Cee as her lips twisted into a grimace. "I just knew someone was going to die."

"I wish you had been wrong."

"I know, but that's what poison will do."

CHAPTER 79

Dr. Herman received the information she had been waiting for, but she hated the results. Someone had deliberately poisoned these people and because of it, a man had died. Taking the business card from her desk drawer, she dialed Wong's number.

"Are you sure Dr. Herman?"

"Yes. There is no doubt. Every person who has been admitted to the hospital with the flu-like symptoms did not have a virus. All of them had been poisoned."

Wong considered what Dr. Herman was saying, but he needed some answers. The first question was, "I thought there was no commonality among these individuals?"

"Yes and no. All of the patients had the same symptoms. When you mentioned poison the CDC interviewed each patient again. Since everyone had hand rashes, we tried to narrow it down to when the patients first noticed it. What we discovered is that everyone had handled golf balls."

Martin wanted a clarification. "But I was under the impression that not everyone golfed. Now, you're saying that even those that had not golfed had been in contact with the poisonous golf balls?"

"That's correct. What we found out was that the non-golfers had found golf balls in their yards or somewhere else. When they picked them up and touched them, they were poisoned."

"What was the poison?"

"Some of the CDC staff went back to the golf courses and they were lucky enough to find some of the poisonous golf balls. After examining them, the poison was a homemade concoction made from baking soda and daffodil bulbs."

Dan was relieved, but still concerned. When he asked his next questions, his mother was on his mind. "Since you know what you're dealing with now, will everyone recover? And, how long will it take?"

Silence entered the phone before Dr. Herman responded. "Those questions are not easy to answer. Everyone has been given the antidote and hopefully everyone will respond positively. Like any illness it will depend on the individual's health and age."

"Well, for everyone's sake, I hope no one else dies. Thank you for calling."

Wong hung up and shared with Martin what Dr. Herman had told him. "We need to obtain a search warrant for Woodward Roberts' house."

CHAPTER 80

Wong called Taylor, the D.A., assigned to the case. He hoped there wouldn't be a problem in obtaining a search warrant. Wong made his request and Taylor told him that he would get back to him. After several hours, Taylor called Wong as promised.

"I'm sorry, but the judge is reluctant to issue a search warrant with only circumstantial evidence."

"Does the judge realize that a person died as a result of this poisoning? In addition, when we questioned Roberts he almost admitted to using golf balls to execute his revengeful act."

"I explained all of that to the judge, but he wanted something more concrete. Without a search warrant, the next best thing I can do is to convene a grand jury."

Wong let out a heavy sigh. "How long will that take?"

"The next grand jury is scheduled for a week from now. I'll let you know the outcome as soon as I receive the verdict."

###

On Friday, the D.A. presented the evidence to the grand jury. Within fifteen minutes, the jurors rendered their verdict.

The D.A. called Wong with the news. "You won't be disappointed. Hands down, the grand jury voted unanimously to indict Woodward Roberts. By two o'clock, I'll have a search and arrest warrant."

With a search and arrest warrant in hand, Wong and Martin, along with back-up police officers, drove to the Roberts' home. Martin parked the car and they climbed out, walking up the sidewalk. They stood at the door while the other officers waited behind them. Martin rang the door bell.

Opening the door, Woody glared. Wong thought Mr. Roberts' would have looked surprised. Instead, his expression was more of aggravation than anything.

Woody could see his reflection in Martin's sunglasses as he

tried staying composed, talking through clenched teeth. "May I help you gentlemen?"

Wong's response was smug. "Mr. Roberts, I have two warrants." He shoved them towards Woody.

The exchange was clumsy. Woody's hands were flying everywhere, trying to catch the papers before they hit the floor. Holding the papers, Woody skimmed quickly over the documents while Wong and the other police officers brushed pass him hard, knocking him off balance.

Woody took his eyes off the papers and yelled, "Hey. Wait a minute."

The number of police officers seemed endless as they stomped inside his house going in different directions and rooms. With swiftness and no regard for anything, they began pulling items out of drawers and overturning sofa and chair pillows.

Woody grabbed his phone and dialed Riley's number. On the second ring, she picked up. "Hello."

"This is Woody Roberts. The police are in my home tearing it apart."

"Did they have a search warrant?"

"Yes."

"I'll be right there. As your lawyer, let me remind you not to say a word. Is that understood?"

CHAPTER 81

Riley must have either been minutes away from Woody's house or she had broken every speed limit posted while driving there. No sooner had Woody hung up the phone than he spotted her rushing up the sidewalk.

Outside of wanting to see Mandy, Woody couldn't have been happier than to lay his eyes on Riley. She greeted him. "Where is the search warrant?"

Woody handed it to her and while she inspected it, he asked, "What's this about?"

Riley glanced up from the documents. "They're looking for daffodil bulbs and baking soda."

Panic began to consume Woody's body as he wondered if this was the time to tell Riley.

"What's wrong Woody?"

"I love flowers and the officers will find the daffodil bulbs that I bought, but have not planted yet. And as far as baking soda was concerned, we have boxes of it. I mean who doesn't use it for home remedies such as deodorizing the refrigerator, brushing your teeth, and God knows what else?"

Riley was about to respond to him when Wong walked up to them. "Mr. Roberts, please turn around. You're under arrest for the murder of Bradshaw Witherspoon."

Wong didn't miss a beat as he placed hand cuffs on Woody. "You have the right to remain silent, you have the right...."

Riley watched Woody go peacefully with the officers. Before he was placed in the police car, he said, "Call Mandy, please."

Riley inhaled and exhaled while she waited for Amanda to pick up. "Hi, Amanda, it's Riley."

"What's up?" Amanda didn't like the sound of Riley's voice. Every nerve in her body tensed.

"Woody has been arrested for murder."

Amanda must have misunderstood. "Riley, please repeat what you just said."

"I'm sorry Amanda, but Woody has been arrested for murder. I'm on my way to the Marion County jail."

"I'm already at the jail. I'll meet you when you get here."

CHAPTER 82

This time when Woody arrived at the police station, he was processed according to standard procedures. His fingerprints and picture were taken with him holding a number in front of him. All he could think about was how he needed to talk to Mandy and that a mistake had been made. He had murdered no one.

Amanda paced while waiting for Riley. Since she was a D.A. and Woody had a lawyer, she thought it was inappropriate to inquire about Woody's arrest, even though she wanted to.

Riley arrived and greeted Amanda. They sat in a corner and talked in low murmurs. "Riley, what is going on?"

She spread her hands to her sides. "Amanda I have no idea. Woody called me and said the police were at your house with a search warrant."

"What were they looking for?"

"They were looking for daffodil bulbs and baking soda. I stayed until they finished the search."

"It's no surprise that they found what they were looking for." Amanda let out a heavy sigh. Silence fell between them. Quickly, the evidence was stacking up against Woody. What had he done?

Amanda was lost in her thoughts. She closed her eyes, made a face and put a finger to the side of her temple, massaging. It was as if she was trying to stop a headache from coming on. Over and over again, the question was, what had Woody done?

Amanda opened her eyes. "I could kill Woody. His behavior had been childish to say the least. His actions might have started out as being harmless, but now he's being indicted for murder. How did this happen?"

Riley's heart went out to Amanda. She had no words to comfort her friend. Besides, she had to be careful in what she said to her about Woody's case. After all he was her client and everything Woody told her was privileged information.

"Woody will be arraigned in the morning. I need to talk to

him. After I finish, you can see him."

To Amanda's surprise Riley didn't spend much time with Woody as she explained. "Woody's tired and wants to rest. He said he would talk to you tomorrow. He also said for you not to worry and that he would be fine."

Riley paused and hugged her friend. "You need to go home and rest. I'll see you in the morning."

Amanda wiped away the falling tear. "But, I want to see him."

"I know, but I think he's embarrassed. I suggest you give him the time he needs to digest everything that's happened."

###

The next morning Woody was arraigned. On the advice of his lawyer, he stated firmly, "Not guilty."

The D.A. and Riley stated their cases clearly regarding the reasons why Woody should or should not be released from jail on bond. Riley fought hard for Woody's release on his own recognizance. At one point, Riley even tried to get the case thrown out for insufficient evidence.

Riley failed on all counts. The reason the judge gave for denying Riley's requests was because of Woody's prior acts, recent arrest, and the possibility of him being a flight risk. The court assigned a trial date. Until then, Woody would remain in jail.

CHAPTER 83

The only public announcement the police made was that they had arrested Woodward Roberts as a suspect with regard to the poisoning of people as well as the death of Bradshaw Witherspoon. Nothing else has been released regarding the particulars. That didn't stop the newspaper and television reporters who eagerly gave their impressions and conclusions about the why's, when's, and how's regarding the arrest.

###

The golf course worker picked up the newspaper and his eyes were immediately drawn to the article about a man who was arrested for possibly poisoning a large number of people as well murder. As he continued reading the column, he learned that the suspect was the same man who had been arrested for committing other golf course crimes.

After reading the article, Lee put the paper down. Shaking his head, he thought, "Had the police arrested the right person?" He wished there had been more details regarding how the individuals had become ill."

He wasn't sure why, but he felt ill-at-ease about the man's arrest. He admonished himself. The police must have had enough evidence to have made the arrest. The question was whether the cause of the illness was from him spreading tainted golf balls throughout The Villages golf courses.

Noisily, he exhaled and smiled recalling what his grandmother used to say. "The guilty always pay and for every action there was a consequence."

The only reason he had helped the homeowner in the first place was because his hours had been cut back. The money had paid his overdue bills and he had put some away for an emergency. Why was money such a necessity, but yet an evil.

Lee couldn't shake the nagging feeling that the homeowner he helped and the man the police arrested was one in the same.

If that was the case he couldn't help but worry whether the homeowner would give him up during the police's interrogation and further investigation of the crime.

The homeowner could easily direct the police towards him. He had made a crucial mistake by giving the homeowner his real name. The question wasn't whether the homeowner would implicate him, but a matter of when.

Rather than wait, Lee packed up his belongings, which wasn't much. Carefully, he surveyed his place, making sure that he had left nothing behind that would lead the police to him. When the place was cleaned, Lee put the trash and his belongings in his truck. He had no destination in mind except to drive as far away from the state of Florida as he could go.

CHAPTER 84

Amanda prayed Woody's guilt or innocence would not be tried by the news media. As quickly as Amanda turned on the television, she turned it off.

To her surprise, Woody's arrest was already the breaking news of the day. This was the last thing his case needed. She knew all too well how the media could easily influence people's opinions and before the facts could be presented, the outcome would be decided.

To compound everything, Woody was refusing to see Amanda. She had no idea why and she couldn't ask because he wouldn't see her. Since his first arrest, both of them had done nothing but cause each other pain and heartache with cruel words and less than loving behavior.

Rather than get discouraged, she sent daily messages to him through Riley. In every written letter, she never failed to say how much she loved him and to be strong. A week before the trial, he agreed to see her.

Amanda approached the glass barrier and when she saw Woody, she was taken aback. The standardized jail issued jumpsuit hung on Woody's tall frame. His sunken cheeks were another indicator of his weight loss.

His eyelids were drooping along with dark circles under his eyes. All signs of fatigue. In such a short period of time, the stress of being in jail and the trial was taking a toll on him.

The glass barrier prevented Amanda from showering Woody with hugs and kisses. From his sad eyes and emotionless expression he seemed as though he needed both. The only affection she could demonstrate was to place her hand against the glass. Woody lingered before doing the same.

A stationary phone hung on each side of the partition. It was their means of communication. Picking up the phone, Amanda couldn't help but notice that Woody was taking his time before lifting it from the cradle.

Forcing a false brightness in her voice, Amanda said, "It's good to see you. How are you doing?"

Clearing his throat, Woody responded, but didn't make eye contact with Mandy. "I'm doing okay. How are you holding up?"

"I'm probably doing as well as you." Amanda brushed away a falling tear. "I'm worried about you, Woody. You look like you've lost weight."

Slowly, he raised his head, his eyes wet. "When I started this, I never intended for anyone to get hurt. I didn't kill anyone. Do you believe me?"

Amanda didn't know what to believe. Several weeks ago, she would have defended him like a protective mother of her children. Then, he was arrested and admitted to being responsible for causing the damage to the golf carts. In her heart, she knew Woody didn't kill anyone, but her training caused her to have doubts.

The silence couldn't have lasted more than several seconds, but it must have seemed like an eternity to Woody. "Well, do you believe I'm innocent?"

Instead of giving Woody the answer he wanted to hear, she hedged. "I believe that you would never hurt anyone intentionally."

Woody huffed. "Thanks for believing in me.

Amanda saw the hurt in his eyes and it made her cringe. "Everything's going to work out."

"How can I believe that when you don't even believe my innocence?" Standing up, Woody hung up the phone. Glaring at Mandy, he turned his back to her and walked to the door. He pressed the wall buzzer.

Tears flowed freely down Amanda's face as she watched Woody wait for the door to open.

CHAPTER 85

Anxiety ridden, Amanda decided that she could no longer just sit on the sidelines and do nothing. She had to help him. Common sense, the law, and Riley would say she shouldn't get involved, but her heart told her differently.

To avoid a conflict of interest regarding her job, she requested a leave of absence. "It will only be until the trial is over." Her supervisor was understanding and told her to take as much time as she needed.

###

Sleep was slow to come as her mind filtered through the facts of Woody's case. In the morning she was tense, exhausted, and edgy.

Since Amanda didn't tell Woody she believed he was innocent, their visits had been strained. Each time she saw Woody, his sad eyes, his taunt jaws and his lack of conversation reminded her of his disappointment in her not being able to say she believed him. She regretted that it had happened and there was nothing she had said since then to repair the damage that had been done.

Regardless of how upbeat and confident Amanda tried to be, emotionally, she felt much like him, hopeless and helpless. That was why she had decided to help.

She wanted to confide in Woody, but decided it was best to keep what she was doing to herself. She was afraid that her involvement would give Woody the impression that she didn't have confidence in Riley. On the other hand, Riley would resent her probing into the case because of her position as well as her being the spouse.

The risks were high, especially if she found anything that might help in proving Woody's innocence. She had to be careful not to taint any evidence she might obtain or her efforts could actually do more harm than good.

The one advantage Amanda had was being a D.A. Discreetly, she would use her power as much as possible to obtain information that Riley may or may not be privy to.

To begin, Amanda created a file. It didn't take long for her to realize there wasn't much evidence in Woody's favor. Glancing over the neighbor interviews Amanda found nothing useful. This wasn't discouraging because past experience told her that most people knew more than they realized.

Perhaps that's where she would begin, but how? Obtaining information from these people would not be an easy feat. For one thing, Amanda's contact with most of her neighbors had been limited. She said hello to them when she was going to or coming from work, but that was about it.

With Mr. Witherspoon's death, Amanda considered going to his memorial service, but she probably would not be welcomed and her attendance would not be appreciated. Considering the pros and cons of going to the service Amanda decided to go, but in disguise.

The long dark wig, designer sunglasses and the wide brimmed hat with the netted black veil covered her face. Glancing in the mirror, Amanda was satisfied with her outward appearance and was ready to go.

CHAPTER 86

Arriving early, Amanda had the opportunity to study the funeral home chapel. Observing the layout, she eyed the pew she needed to sit in if she were to see whomever was coming and going without looking too obvious or suspicious.

With that settled, she strolled up front. Her palms were sweaty, nervous that someone might recognize her. As she stood viewing into the open casket, a woman joined her.

"His death was so unnecessary." Amanda didn't want to get into a conversation about Witherspoon's death. Rather than acknowledge the woman, she said nothing, turned and left the woman's side.

A large lump lodged in Amanda's throat as she extended her hand to Mrs. Witherspoon. "I'm so sorry for your loss." She met Amanda's comment with a nod and wet eyes.

Not knowing what else to say, Amanda moved on to the next family member, mumbling words of sympathy. When there wasn't anyone else to greet, Amanda was glad she had no other condolences to give.

Relief was the word Amanda thought when she walked to a pew and sat down, at the end of the row, close to the wall. This way she would not have to move when others began to sit down.

The chapel filled up quickly and Amanda couldn't tell who was a neighbor or relative. While she was in thought, a woman had sat down beside her and was quite talkative.

"This was such a shame. It didn't have to happen. The police should have taken quicker action to investigate whether the sick people were victims of a crime or was it just an outbreak of a virus."

Eyeing the chubby woman, Amanda couldn't believe it. The woman was Mrs. Tyson. She and her husband had visited Woody when he was in the hospital. When Woody talked about the couple, he had nicknamed them, Mrs. Santa Claus and Mr. Rogers.

Although Amanda had only met the couple once, she could tell she was a busy body, but had an eye for detail. Amanda hoped Mrs. Tyson did not remember her.

From the woman's expression, she was waiting for Amanda to comment on Mr. Witherspoon's death. Amanda leaned close to Mrs. Tyson, trying not to make direct eye contact with her and kept her voice low. "I didn't know him well." Amanda couldn't believe what she said next. "I…I…I'm new to the neighborhood."

The woman held out her hand. "It's nice to meet you. I'm Cee Cee Tyson. This is my husband, Les. We live across the fairway from the Witherspoon's.

Amanda was polite and reminded herself to volunteer little or no information, especially to this woman. Mrs. Tyson might be elderly, but she was sharp. Besides, she couldn't forget that her focus was to gather information, not to give it.

"The Witherspoons liked to cruise. They just returned from one. From what I understand Mr. Witherspoon loved to golf." Cee paused. "By any chance, do you live on the golf course?"

"No, I don't." Amanda had to think fast. "I live one street over from the golf course."

"You have no idea how lucky you are." Cee turned her body towards Amanda, moved her eyeglasses further down on her nose and squinted. "You seem vaguely familiar. Have we met before?"

"I don't think so." Amanda didn't want to stray too much from the truth. "As I stated earlier, we're new to The Villages."

"Um…well, welcome to The Villages. Just be glad you didn't buy a house on the golf course."

"Why is that?"

"I'll tell you later. The minister is about to start the service."

A few relatives stood up and said a few things, but the majority of people who shared stories and memories about Mr. Witherspoon were his golfing buddies and neighbors. According to everyone, Mr. Witherspoon was a nice guy, liked by everyone.

The service ended and before anyone began to leave, a woman made an announcement. "There will be a repast at the Mulberry Recreational Center."

Amanda was taking a chance, but decided to attend the repast, hoping to learn something. By the time she arrived at the recreation center, the parking lot was almost full to capacity. She drove around several times before she spotted an empty space in the back.

"Perhaps this is a sign that I shouldn't go in." Amanda admonished herself. "You have no choice but to go in if you're going to help Woody."

Before getting out of the car, she took a quick glance in the mirror. So far, no one had recognized her and she hoped to keep it that way. That meant avoiding Mrs. Tyson as much as possible.

Entering the recreation center, Amanda glanced around, trying to find an escape route. It was too late as Mrs. Tyson rushed up to her. "Hi, again."

"Hello, Mrs. Tyson."

"Please, please, call me Cee, everyone else does. I'm glad you came. What did you say your name was again?"

Amanda gave a forced smile. She had hoped not to give anyone her name. At least before she attended the service she had decided on a name. "My name is Alice Willard."

"Willard, Willard. I thought I knew most of the neighbors. That name doesn't sound familiar and I don't recall that name being on the neighborhood roster list."

Cee threw up her hand. "It doesn't matter besides at my age I can barely remember my name."

Amanda thought, you might fool some people, but you're as sharp as a knife. She's going to have to be careful about what she says and how she asks questions.

Grabbing Amanda's arm, Cee gushed. "You have to try one of my oatmeal cookies. Everyone says that I make the best cookies and that I should get a patent for them." She laughed. "Who knows, maybe I will and sell them, like the Famous

Amos Cookies."

Amanda followed, trying not to stumble as Cee dragged her to the refreshment table. Cee picked up two cookies, a napkin, and filled a paper cup with punch and handed both to Amanda.

"Thank you." Amanda took a bite of the cookie. Cee waited for Amanda's assessment.

"These are good." Amanda took another bite. "In fact, these are better than those you buy at the bakery."

Cee puffed out her chest with pride. "I'm glad you like them."

Amanda finished the second cookie and took a sip from the paper cup. As she wiped her mouth with the napkin, she was thinking how to form her question to Cee.

"Uh…I'm curious. You stated earlier that I should be happy that we didn't buy a house on the golf course. Why is that?"

Cee's hands became animated as she explained. "Where should I start? The rude golfers, broken windows, trampled landscaping, should I go on?"

"I had no idea."

"Oh it's something, but at least we had one neighbor who cared enough to take action against the golfers. You do know about Mr. Roberts, don't you?"

Amanda hoped she was convincing. "I'm not sure I know who you're talking about."

CHAPTER 87

Cee's eyes widened, looking at Amanda as if she was an alien. "You must be kidding. Don't you read the newspaper or listen to the daily TV or radio news?"

Cee waited for some sort of acknowledgement, but Amanda said nothing. Mr. Roberts is the man who the police dubbed as the Golf Course Menace."

Again, Cee waited to see if Amanda would say anything. When she didn't, she continued, "Anyway, the police arrested him for the flat tire incidents and he got off with a slap on the hand. Now, I'm sure the police are sorry they didn't put him in jail and throw away the key."

"Why is that?"

Cee shook her head. "They had to arrest him again. He was the one who caused all those people to be sick which lead to the death of Mr. Witherspoon."

Amanda's hand flew to her throat. "Do you believe that?"

"No, I don't and I'm probably one of the few. I think it was an accident. I don't know for sure, but he might have been trying to give the golfers a strong warning and nothing else."

"Then you don't think Mr. Roberts' actions were intentional?"

"No, I don't. The man who died was what some people would refer to as collateral damage."

Cee tried to clarify. "What I'm trying to say, and not doing a very good job of it, is that we live in a retirement community. I'm old just like Mr. Witherspoon was. It's hard to be sympathetic about someone who was probably ready to go on the other side anyway."

Amanda gasped. Cee couldn't be serious? How would she feel if someone killed her or led her to an early death? Amanda wanted to respond, but didn't know what to say.

Cee broke into Amanda's thoughts. "Let me introduce you to some of our other neighbors."

Like a dog on a leash, Cee pulled Amanda along from

neighbor to neighbor. Some of the individuals made faces and shifted uncomfortably as Cee introduced Amanda while providing little tidbits about their marital status, church they attended, what they did before they retired, where they moved from, the type of house they lived in and the activities they liked.

Amanda was amazed at how much Cee knew about everyone. She was someone Amanda would like to talk to again, but she knew that would not happen. Cee was more than just a nosy neighbor and it wouldn't take her long to figure out who she really was.

"Cee, it's been a long day…." Before Amanda could finish, Cee's husband had joined them.

"Cee, darling, I think we should be going. This has been a long day and I'm tired."

"Okay, Les."

Before Les and Cee left, Cee went inside her purse and withdrew a business card. "Here's my telephone number. Give me a call sometime Alice and we can do lunch."

CHAPTER 88

Cee and Les watched Amanda walk out the recreation center's door. "There are no Willards living in our neighborhood. I don't know who she is, but she isn't Alice Willard."

Les shrugged. "Then who is she?"

"I'm not sure." Cee snickered. "One thing for sure, the next time she needs to conceal her identity, she should consult an expert. The cheap wig reminded me of the ones sold at Halloween."

They were walking to their car when Cee continued analyzing the woman. "The oversized sunglasses, the large hat with the veil covering her face, they were all over the top. That's what made me wonder why was she trying to hide her identity? There's no doubt in my mind that she didn't want anyone to know who she was."

"But, who do you think she was?"

"I'm not sure, but whoever she was, she was trying to pump me for information. I gave her just enough tidbits to make her curious. If she wants to learn more she will have to call me. That's why I gave her my card."

"Do you think she'll call you?"

"If she's smart, she won't because I'll be the one asking the questions and obtaining information."

As Les drove home, he and Cee continued to talk about the mystery woman. When Les pulled into the garage and before they climbed out, Cee exclaimed, "Whoopee! I know who the woman was?"

"Well, don't leave me in suspense. Who was she?"

"She was Amanda Roberts."

Les cocked his head to the side. "Are you sure?"

"Yes. From the minute I sat down next to her, there was something familiar about her. At the time, I couldn't put my finger on it. I'm telling you it was Amanda Roberts."

"Why do you think she would go to all that trouble to disguise herself?"

Hearing Les' question, Cee wanted to holler in frustration. Les just didn't get it. Patiently, she explained. "She knew people would be talking and maybe even be upset that she would attend the memorial service, so she came in disguise."

Cee slapped her forehead. "She was there in hopes of finding something that could be used to help prove her husband's innocence."

Les wasn't as convinced as Cee. "Maybe, she wanted to show her support, but suspected people wouldn't want her there. Then again, maybe she didn't want to upset the family and felt her presence would have taken away from the service."

"I agree with everything you've said, but it was still dishonest on her part. If she had come as herself, some people might have made some unkind remarks, but for the most part, I think people would have understood. Come on, who did she fool?"

Les didn't comment. He could only think about his own circumstances. If Cee were in jail, he would do everything he could to help her. His heart went out to Amanda Roberts. Her husband was being accused of murder and she probably felt helpless. He was trying to remember a saying something about desperate times call for desperate measures.

"Les, are you okay?"

"Yes, it's just that I feel sorry for both of the Roberts. I can understand how he wanted revenge, but his actions have affected both of their lives."

Les wanted to tell Cee, but didn't, "You should think about some of your antics and how it would affect us if you were ever caught." Constantly, Les worried about Cee and what she was capable of doing when it involved revenge or proving that she was right.

Cee interrupted Les' thoughts. "We'll be at the court house every day. Who knows, maybe I'll be called for jury duty."

"Yeah or you could be called as a witness."

CHAPTER 89

Attending the service had been a waste of Amanda's time. In reality she had learned nothing that could help Woody. The day did have one shining moment and that was Cee Tyson. After talking to her, Amanda was convinced Riley should talk to her. Before Amanda changed clothes, she dialed her number.

"Hey, girl. How are things going?"

Riley was surprised at Amanda's upbeat tone. Understandably, Riley knew how worried and disheartened she was about Woody's plight. "How are you?"

"I'm better than what I was."

Riley had to say what was on her mind. "Rumor has it that you took a leave of absence."

Although Riley did not want to jeopardize their friendship, she felt compelled to give Amanda some advice. "I thought you would want to keep as busy as possible rather than have idle hours doing nothing."

"You're probably right, but I wasn't being productive at work. All I could think about was Woody and perhaps there is something I could do to help. Besides, I need…no, I want to be in court every day. Woody needs my support."

Riley didn't miss the "help" reference Amanda made regarding Woody. "Tell me you're not doing any investigating on your own."

Amanda didn't answer right away. She could lie, but Riley would know it. She hedged, "I would never do anything to jeopardize Woody's case and you know that."

"I know how hard it is standing on the sidelines not being able to do anything, but you have to for Woody's sake. Now, what have you been up to?"

"Well, don't get mad, but I attended Mr. Witherspoon's memorial service."

Amanda kept talking. "I wore a disguise. I don't think anyone recognized me. I have to admit I didn't learn anything new, but I think it's worth talking to Les and Cee Cee Tyson."

Riley did not hide her annoyance. "Amanda, you need to stay out of this. I know you want to help, but this could backfire." Riley paused and gave Amanda a warning. "If you get any leads, call me and I'll follow-up on them."

"Okay. I think I have a lead and you need to follow-up. The police interviewed the Tysons, but I think you need to talk to them again. I think they know more than what they're saying."

Chapter 90

Two weeks before the trial and the firm of Lewis and Lewis had found nothing to prove Woody Roberts' innocence. Riley read over the police interview reports again.

Nothing in them gave her reason to believe that Les and Cee Tyson had any additional information that the police didn't already gather. Since Amanda was adamant about talking to the Tysons, she called them.

Les was disturbed by the call from Riley Lewis. Unlike Cee, he did not welcome the meeting with her. Les was glad he had answered the phone and talked to Ms. Lewis. Cee would have loved to have gone to Ms. Lewis' office, but he asked her to come to their home.

The doorbell startled Les. When he opened the door, he was surprised at the woman standing before him. She was a small-statured woman and looked more like a teenager than an adult. He remembered a saying his grandmother used to say, *"Never judge a shoe's comfort by its cost."* Les was sure that Ms. Lewis' young appearance made her opponents underestimate her abilities.

"Please come in, Ms. Lewis." Les extended his hand and was caught off guard by her firm handshake.

"Please call me Riley."

Les yelled, "Cee. Cee, Ms. Lewis is here."

Cee joined them, her face was red. "Hello."

She wiped her hands on her apron. "I'm Cee Cee Tyson, but please call me Cee. Please excuse me for a minute. When you arrived, I was about to take some cookies out of the oven. I'll be right back."

Les led Riley to a room and told her to have a seat. They sat in silence as Riley glanced around. It was furnished with a loveseat, television, two reclining chairs, and two book cases filled with books and photos. The walls were painted a warm, light yellow and the Thomas Kincaid oil paintings added a comfortable, homey feeling.

When Cee rejoined them, she was carrying a tray with cookies and three glasses on it. "I hope you like sweet tea." Cee set the tray down and handed Riley a glass and a small plate of cookies.

"You'll enjoy my wife's homemade cookies." Les continued, "You can't find many women who make homemade anything anymore. Oh well, I'm glad Cee didn't give up making cookies from scratch."

Mr. Tyson's rambling caused Riley to wonder why he was so nervous. Maybe his uneasiness was because she was representing someone who was accused of murder. While they ate cookies and drank tea, their conversation was about the weather, The Villages, and where they had moved from.

Riley took the last bite of the cookie and wiped her mouth with the napkin. "Thank you for meeting with me. As I told your husband, I represent Mr. Woody Roberts. Are you familiar with the case?" Riley looked from Les to Cee.

"My goodness! Who doesn't know about the case? In fact, I don't know how you're going to find people to sit on the jury."

Riley was curious. "Why do you say that?"

"From talking to our neighbors as well as people in the grocery store, restaurants, and church, most people have already decided on his guilt or innocence."

"Do you really believe that Mrs....Cee?"

"Well, yeah. I bet most people living on the golf course would find him innocent without considering what he had done." Cee paused. "Technically, Mr. Roberts committed a crime, but I think the man's death was what the military would call, *"collateral damage."* What I mean is that Mr. Witherspoon was in the wrong place at the wrong time."

Riley was surprised at Cee's attitude, but wasn't surprised that people had begun forming opinions and taking sides. Any time the media starts covering a story and it gets national attention, it's expected.

Riley folded her hands in a tent and leaned forward. "Do you know of anyone who might have put the golf balls on the golf course other than Mr. Roberts?"

Nervously, Les and Cee laughed. In unison they said, "Yeah, everyone who lives on the golf course."

For over an hour, Riley asked Les and Cee specific questions about what they knew or what others might know and it amounted to nothing. All they had were opinions and gossip. They had no concrete evidence that could help Woody.

Although Riley left with the same information she already had, she was pleased with the interview. The Tyson's had boosted Riley's confidence in that she could raise reasonable doubt in the jury's mind.

Riley didn't have to include Cee Tyson on her witness list since the prosecution already had her on theirs. Riley wondered why. From what she could tell, Cee would help Woody's case more than the other side. Riley was pleased thinking about Cee on the witness stand. The woman would not be able to stop herself in stating how anyone owing a house on the golf course had issues with golfers.

CHAPTER 91

Not one seat was empty in the court room. Smiling, Riley recalled Cee Tyson's words. *"Lots of people are interested in this case. Most of them have already decided Mr. Roberts' guilt or innocence."*

When Riley spotted Woody, he was dressed in his own business suit, the prison clothes abandoned for a few hours. The suit confirmed what Amanda had told her. Although Riley had numerous meetings with Woody it wasn't until now that she noticed how much weight he had lost. In addition to the thinness, dark circles were under his eyes and his overall appearance resembled a man who had not slept in days.

Riley took her seat beside Woody. When she patted his hand, it felt frail and he was shaking. Instead of looking at her, his head was turned, his eyes focused on the crowd. Turning, she realized why. He was searching for Amanda and when he found her, Riley noticed his shoulders relaxed.

Before Riley resumed her position, she couldn't miss seeing Les and Cee Tyson. They were sitting directly behind Amanda. They waved at Riley.

Shelton Taylor was the D.A. and had a record for winning most of his cases. This had become a high profile case and he would love to add this to his wins.

During the selection process, Taylor challenged each person who owned a house or had owned a house on a golf course. Riley was torn between objecting to anyone who was or had been a golfer. These individuals may or may not have understood Woody's motivation. The only thing that was going to free Woody would be reasonable doubt. Riley had to find a way to create it. After two days a jury was selected.

The diverse makeup of the men and women selected to serve met Riley's expectations. The final selection was: five women, ranging from thirty to sixty and seven men from their middle twenties to over seventy. Three of the women were married and working professionals. The other two women were single; one was a waitress and one a beauty shop owner. The men consisted of three retirees: a travel agent, an accountant, a bus driver, and a fast food worker. The alternates were both retired: one was a female retired government worker and the other was a male bookstore owner.

CHAPTER 92

Every seat was occupied in the court room. The murmuring voices sounded louder than normal. The noise halted when the deep, commanding voice of the bailiff stated firmly, "All rise. The Honorable Judge Baker is presiding." The judge entered, banged his gavel on the desk to signal the beginning of the trial.

The prosecution as well as Riley's witness list was short. Riley was still undecided as to whether Woody would take the stand. The trial should last no longer than three days.

The first witness was Lieutenant Dan Wong. He was sworn in and took a seat in the witness box. The questioning was about his background and outstanding police record. Riley glanced at the jury box.

With a witness a lawyer has to create a balance or you lose your jurors' attention. She understood the importance of establishing Wong's credibility, but Taylor needed to move on because some of the jurors were yawning while others were nodding.

"Lieutenant Wong, please explain why Woodward Roberts was arrested for the murder of Bradshaw Witherspoon?" That question made the jurors look up and pay attention.

"Primarily because Mr. Roberts had been arrested recently for...."

"Objection, Your Honor. Mr. Roberts' previous arrest has no bearing on this case."

Taylor said, "Your Honor, it has everything to do with this case. It shows motive."

Judge Baker overruled. "You may answer the question."

"As I was saying, Mr. Roberts was arrested and he admitted to being the Golf Course Menace. For those of you that don't know about that case, Mr. Roberts was responsible for spreading screws and nails on golf courses throughout The Villages, causing damage to golf carts."

"Thank you for the explanation. Now, why was Mr. Roberts arrested for the murder of Mr. Witherspoon?"

"He was the logical person because of his prior arrest. Also, daffodil bulbs and baking soda were found in his home."

"Why were the daffodil bulbs important?"

"The Villages Hospital determined that the unexplained illness was caused by daffodil bulbs which were poisonous."

"Thank you, Lieutenant." When Taylor finished, he sneered smugly at Riley.

CHAPTER 93

Riley stood, buttoned her suit jacket and stood behind the defense table. "Lieutenant Wong, is it possible that someone else could have committed the crime?"

"No, because…"

"Just answer the question Lieutenant Wong. Did you look at anyone besides Mr. Roberts?"

"No."

"Weren't there other homeowners just as angry as Mr. Roberts when it came to the golfers and their behavior?"

"I don't know."

"Isn't it true that Ms. Tyson tried to organize the neighborhood into forming a group to combat the problems with golfers?"

"Yes, I heard something about that."

Riley was feeling more in control. "Did you follow-up by interviewing any of these individuals?"

Lieutenant Wong lowered his head, saying nothing.

"Your, Honor, please instruct Lieutenant Wong to answer the question." The judge didn't have to warn Lieutenant Wong.

Through clenched teeth, Wong responded. "We did not interview any other neighbors that owned houses on the golf course."

Riley smiled as she went for the jugular. "So, you don't know whether these individuals had alibis or arguments with any of the golfers and could therefore have committed the crime?"

Taylor jumped to his feet. "Objections, Your Honor."

"I withdraw the question. I don't have any further questions for Lieutenant Wong." Riley turned her back and returned to her seat. This time it was Riley's turn to be smug.

"Mr. Taylor," the judge said, "You may reexamine."

"Thank you, Your Honor." He rose and stood behind the prosecution's table. "Lieutenant Wong, how long have you been a police officer?"

"Almost fifteen years."

"In your experience, why did you focus your investigation on Mr. Roberts and no one else?"

"Mr. Roberts was our primary focus because he had just been arrested and admitted to committing the golf course crimes. It seemed plausible that if Mr. Roberts was capable of taking revenge on golf carts then his next target might be the golfer."

"Objection," said Riley.

"Sustained," said the judge, but the damage was done as Riley glanced at the jurors' facial expressions and body language.

"Thank you, Lieutenant Wong. I have no further questions."

"The witness may step down." The judge glanced at his watch. "The hour is getting late. We will resume tomorrow morning at nine o'clock." He banged his gavel. "Court is adjourned."

"All rise!" shouted the bailiff.

CHAPTER 94

The next morning, the trial started off with Taylor calling Dr. Olivia Herman. Actually, Riley had expected her to be the first witness rather than Lieutenant Wong. Regardless, Riley didn't expect any surprises regarding the doctor's testimony.

Taylor's questions began with asking Dr. Herman about her background and position at the hospital. Boredom made some jurors twisting in their seats while others were looking down or scribbling on tablets.

After what seemed an eternity, Taylor finally asked the most pertinent question to his examination. "Dr. Herman, why did it take the hospital so long to test the sick individuals for poison?"

"Well, it's complicated. When an individual comes to the hospital with certain symptoms, unnecessary tests aren't run unless there is evidence for doing so. Usually, doctors try to make a diagnosis by process of elimination."

"So why did you test for poison?"

"It was the urging from Lieutenant Wong who told me that the police had received an anonymous tip. The person indicated that the sick patients might have been poisoned."

"And, what did your tests reveal?"

Dr. Herman glanced at the jurors. "The individuals were indeed poisoned."

"Could you tell us what type of poison was used?"

"Yes, the poison was a homemade compound of daffodil bulbs and baking soda."

Taylor took his time asking the next question. "How did you identify the poison?"

"The autopsy was inconclusive as to the type of poison, but we were lucky to obtain several golf balls that were still covered with the substance. From the lab's examination of the balls, confirmation was made regarding the type of poison."

"Did the poison kill Mr. Witherspoon?"

"From the autopsy report, I would say that the poison contributed to Mr. Witherspoon's death."

"Thank you, Dr. Herman."

CHAPTER 95

Before the doctor stepped down from the witness stand, the judge said, "Your witness, Ms. Riley."

"Dr. Herman, I only have a few questions. Has anyone else died from the poisoned golf balls?"

"No."

Riley crossed her fingers as she asked her next question. "How are the people that were poisoned doing?"

"First of all, everyone that was sick was admitted to the hospital for tests and observances. Everyone was released and from the follow-up visits, I can say all patients are recovering without any problems."

"Did any of these patients have any other medical problems such as heart or Diabetes?"

"Yes."

"Did any of these individuals die? More importantly, have they recovered? Again, Riley had no idea how Dr. Herman was going to answer the question.

"To your first question, no one died except for Mr. Witherspoon and as I stated earlier, everyone is recovering without complications."

"Thank you, Dr. Herman. I have no other questions. Riley glanced at the jurors. Some were busy taking notes. That may be a good sign.

"Mr. Taylor, you may call your next witness."

"Your Honor, the next witness is Derek Huey."

Riley watched Mr. Huey take the stand. According to Woody, the man worked in the Golf USA Pro Shop, but that was the only contact he had with this man. Riley's staff did some research and verified what Woody had said. She wasn't sure the significance of his testimony.

After the man was sworn in, he took a seat. Riley glanced at Woody. He seemed nervous as he played nervously with the pencil.

"Mr. Huey, where do you work?"

"I'm a sales representative for the Golf USA Pro Shop located on Route 466."

"How do you know Mr. Woodward Roberts?"

"He's a frequent customer."

Taylor walked to the prosecutor's table and picked a piece of paper. "Your Honor, this is Exhibit 1." The judge glanced at it and handed it back to Taylor.

"Mr. Huey, can you tell the court what this is?"

Mr. Huey took the exhibit and looked at it. "This is a copy of a sales slip for 350 golf balls."

"Can you tell the court who placed and paid for the order?"

"Mr. Woodard Roberts."

The courtroom gallery erupted into loud chatter. The judge banged his gavel several times. "May there be order in the court." Louder, he barked, "I said, order in the court."

Once quiet had been restored, Taylor said, "Thank you." He smiled. "Your Honor, I have no other questions."

Since Taylor didn't ask the question, Riley exhaled and took a chance. "Mr. Huey how many people, besides Mr. Roberts, placed an order for large quantities of golf balls?"

"I reviewed the sales slips for the past three months and I couldn't find anyone else besides Mr. Roberts."

Mr. Huey's comment hung in the air like the odor from cooking cabbage and the jurors smelled it. Riley had shot herself in the foot. Taylor had set the trap and without much bait, she had taken it. She knew better than to enter into territory where she had no or little information.

"Thank you Mr. Huey. Your Honor, I have no other questions for this witness."

CHAPTER 96

Unfortunately for Riley, two days into the trial and it had ended badly. From Amanda and Woody's expressions, Riley knew there wasn't much she could say to bolster their confidence or moral. Her defense of reasonable doubt was dissolving quickly into thin air.

Mr. Huey's testimony was the type of surprise Riley hated. Woody had been questioned many times about Mr. Huey and he couldn't think of anything that would be significant about his testimony. How had Woody forgotten about ordering and buying that many golf balls? Mr. Huey's testimony had hurt Woody's credibility.

Before Woody was taken back to jail, Riley requested a meeting. She needed to confer with Woody. When the door closed, Riley did not hide her annoyance. "Now that we know that you bought large quantities of golf balls, what else haven't you told me?"

Woody ran his hands through his hair. "Listen, I forgot I bought them. If you go through their sales slips, you'll see I have been buying large amounts of golf balls for years." His explanation was not helping.

"Let me clarify. Some of the golf balls are for my personal use. Anyone who is a golfer loves to receive golf balls. I give away a dozen at a time for birthdays, anniversaries, door prizes and any other occasion. Surely, I'm not the only person who buys large quantities of golf balls."

Riley didn't intend for her words to be harsh. "Did you not hear what Mr. Huey said? You were the only person who bought large quantities of golf balls from that particular store."

"What about other stores? Did anyone check?"

"To be honest, no we did not. Why? We didn't know about you buying large quantities of golf balls."

"Then, are you going to check?"

"Woody, we don't have time and I doubt if the judge will give us an extension because I should have been told about this by my client." She stood up and turned her back to Woody.

"I hate surprises." She sat back down. "The prosecution has two more witnesses, Cee Tyson and Lenny Harper. Do you have any idea why they are being called or what they might say?"

Immediately, Woody responded regarding Cee Tyson. "I met the woman when she and her husband visited me in the hospital after I was injured by the stray golf ball. Other than that, I don't know the woman."

Woody bit on his lower lip. He didn't know how much to tell her or what she might know about Lenny.

"Lenny Harper…" He ran his hand over his face and hesitated. "Well, he and Amanda had an affair."

Riley prided herself in having a poker face, but hearing what Woody just said, she hoped her mouth was not hanging open. The affair surprised her. Amanda never mentioned it to her. What matter was that Woody told her before she learned about it in the court room.

CHAPTER 97

After the court room had been called to order, Taylor called Lenny Harper to the stand. He was sworn in and took a seat.

"Mr. Harper, how do you know Mr. Roberts?"

"We took golf lessons together…well…actually there were a total of eight men who took golf lessons together."

"Do you know Mr. Roberts' wife?"

"Objection, Your Honor. How is any of this relevant?"

"Mr. Taylor, I have to agree with Ms. Lewis."

"Your, Honor if you will allow me a little leeway I'll get to the relevance very shortly."

"Make it quick, Mr. Taylor." The judge said, "Mr. Harper you may answer the question."

Lenny shifted in the chair and cleared his throat. "Mrs. Roberts and I had an affair."

"When Mr. Roberts found out, what did he do?"

Again, Lenny cleared his throat and glanced down when he responded. "He…Mr. Roberts hit me." Lenny hurried on before Taylor could stop him. "But, he reacted like any husband would have after discovering his wife had an affair. I know.…"

Quickly, Taylor tried to stop Mr. Harper. "Your, Honor, tell the witness to answer only the questions that I ask." The judge did as Taylor had requested.

After that outburst, Taylor wanted Mr. Harper off the stand. "Thank you, Mr. Harper. I have nothing else."

Riley sat for a few minutes and her thoughts were interrupted by the judge. "Ms. Lewis, do you have any questions for this witness?"

Riley declined. Nothing would be gained by asking any questions of this witness. The only point Taylor might have proven was that Woody had a temper. She believed that Mr. Harper helped Woody when he defended him of his actions.

CHAPTER 98

The judge called a recess until after lunch. Riley wished she knew what Cee Tyson might say. In Riley's opinion, she was unpredictable and could not be controlled. She was hoping that her testimony would help Woody more than it would hurt. Time would only tell.

The court room was called to order. With Mrs. Tyson sworn in she approached the witness box. Riley watched the woman take the stand. Although Mrs. Tyson was dressed in a two-piece navy blue pant suit, Riley couldn't help but think about the first time they met and how much she thought she resembled Mrs. Santa Claus.

Taylor began slowly. He asked Mrs. Tyson a series of questions involving her relationship with Woody and how she came to know him. Taylor had established the ground work he had intended and proceeded.

"Can you explain what it's like owning a house on the golf course?"

Pushing back from the table, Riley was ready to object. She hesitated and decided to wait and hear what Cee had to say.

Smiling, Mrs. Tyson turned her body in the direction of the jurors. It seemed as if she wanted the entire jurors' attention before she answered.

"Well, this is our second home and living on the golf course was new to me and my husband, Les. The view is beautiful, but what we didn't expect was the golfers' loud chatter, laughter, and most of all the balls that are constantly hit into our yard."

She paused. "Did I mention how these balls break windows? Unfortunately, the golfers don't pay for the damages and our insurance company won't cover the damages. I forgot to tell you how the golfers destroy the landscaping by trampling on the flowers and shrubs while searching for their golf ball."

Mrs. Tyson threw her hands up in the air. "It is a situation the homeowner can't win, especially when the golfers argue with you."

Riley was surprised at how much leeway Taylor was allowing Mrs. Tyson in answering questions. She was delighted. Mrs. Tyson was creating reasonable doubt.

Taylor nodded and inquired further. "What did the homeowners do about the golfers?"

Cee continued talking to the jurors. "Each homeowner dealt with the problem as they saw fit." She paused.

"Les and I tried to organize our neighbors because there is strength in numbers. Unfortunately, no one wanted to take on the golfers. In fact, the attitude was, The Villages is a golfing community."

She hissed. "And the police, they were useless. They said we should take the golfers to small claims court or have a mediator settle our differences. We pay taxes like everyone else and this is how the police treated our complaints."

She spread her hands out. "Now, can you understand why Mr. Roberts did what he did?"

CHAPTER 99

Riley didn't want to appear as if she was picking on the elderly so when she objected, she used a syrupy voice. "Objection, your Honor. Please explain to Mrs. Tyson that she should only answer the questions being asked of her.

Before the judge could explain the point to Cee she asked, "Isn't that what I'm doing, Your Honor?"

The judge smiled. "Yes, you are, Mrs. Tyson, and you're doing just fine. Unless you're asked the question, please try not to add any additional information."

Cee shrugged. She wanted to make sure the jurors understood what the homeowners were facing and if she had to add information, she would.

"Mrs. Tyson, how did this make you feel?"

Riley was taken aback at Taylor's line of questioning. Depending on Mrs. Tyson's answer, this could be a positive on her side. She leaned forward and listened.

"I guess most of the homeowners, including me and Les were upset that no one cared. Basically, we had to fight our own battle."

Cee hurried on before anyone could stop her. "It seemed to me that Mr. Roberts was justified in what he did and I applaud him for having the courage to retaliate against the golfers."

Riley was on her feet, but the damage had been done. "Your, Honor."

The judge warned. "Mrs. Tyson, may I remind you to answer only the question asked."

"I'm sorry, Your Honor, but I'm trying to help the jurors understand what might have motivated Mr. Roberts into doing what he did."

The judge tried to mask his smile. He looked at Taylor, who shrugged.

The judge thought, "No matter what he said, Mrs. Tyson was going to say what she wanted." The judge tried again. "Mrs. Tyson, I understand what you're saying, but try to confine your answers only to the questions being asked."

Cee smiled. "I'll try. I'm just trying to do my civic duty."

Taylor said, "No more questions. Mrs. Tyson, thank you."

Cee was about to stand up from the chair when the judge said, "Mrs. Tyson, you're not finished. Ms. Lewis has the right to ask you questions."

CHAPTER 100

Riley noticed Mrs. Tyson's demeanor change upon hearing what the judge told her. The charming expression that had covered her face had disappeared.

Riley stood up and walked toward the witness stand. Despite that grandmotherly appearance, Riley bet Mrs. Tyson could be like a shark smelling blood.

"Mrs. Tyson, since you and the other homeowners were just as upset about the golfers as Mr. Roberts, is it fair to say that any one of you might have planted those poisonous golf balls on the golf course?"

Taylor jumped to his feet. "Objection, Your Honor."

"I withdraw the question." Riley smiled.

"Mrs. Tyson, did you ever have a conversation with Mr. Roberts about the golfers' behavior and what could be done about them?"

Cee didn't answer immediately. She crunched up her face. "I witnessed a ball hitting Mr. Roberts' head, but I don't think Les or I ever talked to him about how he might get even with the golfers."

She shook her head. "No, I never talked to him."

Riley tried another question. "Mrs. Tyson, did you ever consider doing anything similar to what Mr. Roberts did?"

"I would never knowingly hurt anyone."

That wasn't quite the response Riley wanted from Mrs. Tyson, but she continued, "Mrs. Tyson, isn't it true that you have used some unusual techniques when you have solved several issues that affected the villas where you used to live?"

"Objection, your, Honor. What does this have to do with...."

Before Taylor could continue, Riley talked over him. "Your, Honor Mrs. Tyson stated that she would never hurt anyone, but I would like to explore that statement."

The judge pondered over Riley's statement. "Ms. Lewis I will allow you to continue with this line of questioning, but I want you to get to the point quickly. Mrs. Tyson, you may answer the question."

"Yes, sir."

"Mrs. Tyson, exactly what was your role in helping the police capture the individuals who were breaking into the villas?"

Riley had no idea if Mrs. Tyson helped the police or not, but her gut told her that she had more to do with the capture of the thieves than anyone knew. She was banking on Mrs. Tyson's ego to tell everyone.

"Oh, dear me." Cee put her hand over her heart. "You're giving me far too much credit. This was a neighborhood effort. We formed a neighborhood watch program that put an end to the break-ins."

"Were the thieves caught?"

"Not right away."

"So, what happened?"

"Your, Honor. Where is this going and what is the relevance to this case?"

"I have to agree with Mr. Taylor, Ms. Lewis."

"Sir, if you'll just give me a minute."

"Hurry along and make your point."

"Mrs. Tyson, what did you do if anything to get these individuals caught?"

Cee was looking at her husband. She had to tell the truth. She had been sworn in. Her tone was defensive when she responded. "If I didn't do something those men would still be breaking into houses. The police had given up!"

She crossed her arms over her chest and huffed. "I had to take matters into my own..." She stopped in mid-air.

"Please Mrs. Tyson explain to everyone exactly what you did.

"I'm not ashamed to say that my methods worked and the criminals were arrested, but I never hurt anyone."

Frustrated, Riley didn't know what to do about Mrs. Tyson. She answers the questions the way she wants to and adds information when it suits her.

Mrs. Tyson stopped and when she continued, her voice had returned to a normal pitch. "My approach when dealing with the golfers was to reason with them. Not that it helped. Then Mr. Roberts had the brilliant idea to put nails and screws on the golf course. I wish I had been as brave as him."

Riley threw her hands up in the air. That was it. She wanted Mrs. Tyson off the stand as soon as possible. From the jurors' expressions, Riley knew that Mrs. Tyson's side comments had done more harm than good.

CHAPTER 101

Again, the day did not end the way Riley had hoped. The prosecution was finished and it was now up to her. After interviewing Mrs. Tyson, Riley realized that she didn't have much of a case.

Riley's witness list was primarily made up of character witnesses. Their testimonies had not helped. The only person who might have helped was Justin Williams, Woody's friend and minister. Unfortunately, that was about it.

The question was whether to put Woody on the stand. Riley's training said, no, but her instincts said, perhaps it would help for him to tell his story. Maybe, one of the jurors would be sympathetic towards anyone having a house on the golf course and the challenges that a homeowner had to endure.

What worried Riley was Woody's temper. She was sure Taylor could and probably would make him lose it. That was a chance she wasn't willing to take.

Riley had hoped to create reasonable doubt because of lack of evidence, however she had been unsuccessful. At one point she even asked the judge to drop all charges because of the lack of proof, but it was futile. The only thing that was going to set her client free was if she were a magician and she had something up her sleeve or could pull something out of a hat.

The options for Riley's client were running out. One alternative she had not explored was a plea bargain. She met with Taylor.

"I've been waiting for you. The best I can do is to offer your client, twenty to life."

Riley doubted that Amanda and Woody would accept it, but she presented it to them. Carefully, Riley explained how much time he could receive if found guilty. It didn't matter. They declined the offer, believing Woody would do better with the jury.

Riley did not comment on their decision or try to persuade them in anyway. This was their life and they had to live with the verdict. It always surprised her when a person in the profession loses all sensibility when a loved one is on trial. The tendency was to forget about logic and that is what she believed had happened to Amanda.

That night Riley did not sleep well. For two hours she would drift off, wake up, glance at the clock, and doze off again. Each time she woke up, she returned to the same dream—the jury's verdict is guilty.

The alarm went off and when Riley climbed out of the bed, she was exhausted and dreading the day. Putting on her make-up, she used it heavily to cover the bags under her eyes.

Recalling the dream, Riley wondered if it was an omen. She hoped it was not. Every time Riley heard the word guilty she associated it with someone being told they have cancer. Sometimes there's a cure and other times it's a death sentence.

Before the court day started, Riley spoke to Woody and Amanda, informing them that she would not put Woody on the stand. Neither of them was happy with her decision. She had to remind them that she was the lawyer.

Court was called to order. "Ms. Lewis, you may continue with your witnesses."

"Your, Honor, the defense rests." With Woody not testifying, Riley caused a rumble throughout the court room.

After a long pause, the judge proceeded. "Mr. Taylor you may begin your closing remarks."

Listening, Riley watched the jury as Taylor skillfully laid out the case against Woody. When Taylor finished, the jurors' faces were solemn, revealing nothing.

Riley rose from her seat. She knew her words would have to connect with at least one juror to make them think, *reasonable doubt*. As Riley made her closing remarks, she walked from one end of the jury box to the other making eye contact with as many jurors that would look at her.

The only time Riley knew she had made some headway was when several of the jurors nodded their heads. The point she made was to compare Woody to people who believed they had the right to bear arms.

Everything was over—the witnesses and closing remarks. Before the jurors left to discuss the case, the judge gave them some last-minute instructions. The men and women filed out of the court room. The time had come and the waiting would begin until the jury rendered their verdict.

CHAPTER 102

While the jury deliberated, Riley and Amanda went to lunch. All lawyers believed that if the jury takes a short time to deliberate, the verdict was usually guilty.

Instead of talking about the trial, Riley and Amanda talked leisurely about everything and nothing of importance. They even talked about the possibility of going to Belk's department store where a huge sale was going on. Those plans were short lived when Riley received a telephone call.

"What's wrong?" Amanda asked when Riley closed her cell phone.

"The jury is back with a verdict."

"Are you kidding me? It's been less than two hours."

"I know. We have to go." They paid the bill and drove back to the court house.

As the jury filed in, Riley watched their faces. The expressions were not promising, especially since none of them would make eye contact with her. No one would even look in her direction. Nervously, Riley shifted in her chair.

The bailiff barked, "All rise."

The judge looked at the jury. "Mr. Foreman, I understand the jury has reached a verdict."

The foreman stood up. "Yes, Your Honor."

The court clerk walked over to the foreman. He handed the written verdict to the clerk. In return, the clerk handed it to the judge who inspected it. He returned it to the clerk for public disclosure. The tension could be felt throughout the courtroom. Everyone was sitting on the edge of their seat, waiting for the verdict to be read.

"Would the defendant please rise," the judge requested.

Glancing at Woody, Riley touched his arm. They stood up, waiting for his fate.

"In the matter of the State versus Woodward Roberts, on the charge of murder in the second degree," the clerk read from the verdict form, "We, the jury, find the defendant: guilty."

Leaning close to Woody, Riley was about to say something to him, but she stopped. His breathing was shallow.

"I can't breathe. He grabbed Riley's hand hard."

Without warning, Riley tried to catch Woody. Instead she watched his body slip from her grip and float to the floor.

Chaos replaced the quietness of the court room. Amanda rushed to Woody's side.

Everyone was talking all at once, offering their assistance. One voice yelled, "Call 911." Another voice shouted, "Is there a doctor in the courtroom?"

CHAPTER 103

Woody was rushed to the hospital. Once again, Amanda found herself pacing. Patiently, along with Riley they were waiting to hear from the doctor regarding Woody's condition.

Amanda was relieved when the doctor said, "He'll be fine. He had a panic attack."

With Woody's collapse, the judge delayed the sentencing hearing for a week.

###

One week later, Riley was sitting beside Woody, waiting his fate. Court was brought to order.

"Mr. Roberts before I render your sentence, Mrs. Witherspoon requested that she be allowed to make a statement to the court."

Mrs. Witherspoon sat in the witness seat. "Thank you Your, Honor. I appreciate you giving me this opportunity." She pulled out a piece of paper and began reading.

"What happened to my husband was a tragedy. What was more of a heartbreak was my husband having stage four Cancer and was told that he had only three months to live. My husband had a wonderful life and he was living on borrowed time." She paused and blew her nose before continuing.

"People cannot take the law into their own hands and what Mr. Roberts did was regrettable. I believe the poison did not cause my husband's death. I forgive Mr. Roberts for his actions and my husband's death was a blessing. He won't have to suffer." She turned to the judge. "Thank you."

The judge nodded his head toward Mrs. Witherspoon. "Thank you for your statement. Mr. Roberts please stand." Woody and Riley stood up.

"The court hopes you're feeling better."

"I'm fine Your, Honor. Thanks for asking."

"Mr. Roberts, you have been found guilty and with the

authority...."

A man's booming voice interrupted the judge. "Mr. Roberts is innocent. He's innocent. I did it."

CHAPTER 104

Riley and Woody turned around to see who was speaking.

"Mr. Roberts is innocent. I did it. I'm the one responsible for poisoning the golfers." The man yelling was Les Tyson.

Cee watched her husband in disbelief. What was he saying? How could he have poisoned those people and why? Everything was a blur. Hard, she yanked on his sleeve, trying to pull him back into his seat.

Forcefully, he pulled away from her. He continued with his outburst. "Mr. Roberts is innocent."

Banging his gavel, the judge bellowed, "Order in the court, order in the court." He paused and stated loudly, "Mr. Taylor and Ms. Lewis, in my chambers and bring that man with you."

Inside the judge's quarters, everyone had taken a seat. He made a tent with his fingers and spoke directly at Les. "Now, can you tell me who you are and why you said Mr. Roberts was innocent?"

"My name is Les Tyson. I'm married to Cee Cee Tyson." He exhaled heavily. "I don't know how to explain what I'm about to say, but I couldn't let an innocent man go to jail for what I've done." He paused and ran his hand over his face.

"Mr. Tyson, take your time. Would you like a glass of water?" asked the judge.

Les shook his head. "I'm fine."

"Just start from the beginning."

"As you heard from my wife, we live on the golf course. Having to deal with the golfers almost daily has taken a toll on me and my wife. For anyone who has not experienced it, we probably sound silly. But, to have your windows broken and your landscape trampled, it begins to feel as if you're been violated on a constant basis. To make matters worse, you have no recourse. Can I have that glass of water after all?"

The judge poured water into a glass and handed it to Les. He took a sip and proceeded. "You heard my wife, she tried everything. We even tried to engage the police, but nothing worked."

Les let out a nervous laugh. "Judge, the hardest part of this is my wife. You don't know her. If I had not done what I did, she would have found a way to do something. To prevent her from hurting someone or someone hurting her, I took matters into my own hands."

Les chewed on his lower lip. "Every day I watched my wife argue with the golfers. Then, she learned that Mr. Roberts had taken matters into his own hands by planting nails and screws on the golf course in order to damage golf carts."

Shaking his head, Les said, "At that point I began to worry about Cee. I knew she would do something. I am so sorry that someone died because of my actions. The daffodil bulbs weren't supposed to kill anyone."

Lowering his voice, Les continued. "According to my research, exposure to it would only cause diarrhea, high temperature, and a rash. Regrettably, I forgot that most of The Villages residents are elderly and have medical conditions."

The judge's chambers fell quiet until the judge spoke, directing his words to Mr. Tyson. "Mr. Tyson, it is never a good idea to take the law into your own hands. I wish you had left this up to the police. Unfortunately, you didn't and now you're under arrest for murder."

CHAPTER 105

With Mr. Tyson's confession, Woody would be released from jail after the paperwork was completed.

Since it would take about thirty minutes to process Woody, Amanda walked over to her office. She was planning a surprise for Woody. She had requested another week of vacation.

When Amanda walked in, everyone congratulated her regarding Woody's release. After receiving the approval of her vacation request, she was about to leave when a co-worker stopped her.

"I wanted to bring you up-to-date regarding Les Tyson's case." The co-worker explained.

"Mr. Tyson had been quite thorough in deciding what poison to use and how to spread the golf balls throughout the various Village golf courses. What the police couldn't figure out and he wouldn't say--how was he able to go around the golf courses without being noticed."

The co-worker ended by saying, "Les continues to say that he did everything by himself. He had no help. The police believe his wife is just as guilty as he is, but they can't prove her involvement."

Amanda agreed. "I'm sure his wife knew about it. In fact, I wouldn't be surprised if she wasn't the mastermind behind the scheme."

The co-worker lowered her voice. "From what I hear, there won't be a trial. As we speak, a plea bargain is being negotiated. I understand that the D.A. in charge was going to be lenient."

"Are you saying Mr. Tyson's not going to do time?"

"I think he'll do time, but it won't be very much. According to the grapevine, the leniency was based on Mrs. Witherspoon's statement and Mr. Tyson's age and health."

"Listen, I have to go. I'm sure Woody's been processed by now. I appreciate you giving me the update."

CHAPTER 106

Woody and Amanda took a vacation in the Bahamas. After two days of sunning on the beach, Woody mustered up enough courage.

"I know you probably don't want to hear this, but when we return to The Villages, let's sell the house. As much as I love the golf course view, I've had enough. With everything that's happened I realize that nothing is going to change the issues between the golfers and the homeowners."

Amanda didn't respond immediately as she flipped through the magazine. Slowly, she closed it and turned to him, smiling. "I agree with you."

"I'm sorry, Amanda for everything. I know what I did was wrong and I almost paid dearly for my actions. Can you ever forgive me?"

Amanda reached over and gave him a kiss.

###

Upon their return, Woody made contact with the real estate office and a "For Sale" sign was placed in the yard. Despite the slow economy, the real estate agent believed the designer home would sell quickly. From her experience, someone is always looking for a house on the golf course.

The first open house was held. As instructed, Woody and Amanda left the premises to give people the opportunity to walk through the house freely and have an open discussion about their likes and dislikes.

The three hours were up and Woody and Amanda returned home. Woody was about to pull into the garage, but a car was parked in front of the house.

Amanda suggested, "Park on the street. Maybe a prospective buyer is still looking at the house."

"That's a good idea." Woody parked the car at the curb. They climbed out and walked up the sidewalk. Before Woody rang the doorbell, they agreed to pretend to be perspective buyers.

A man, not the agent, opened the house. The man greeted them. "Hello. I don't think the real estate agent heard the doorbell. You're welcomed to come in, but I think the open house is over."

"Thank you."

"The last time I saw the agent, she was out on the lanai."

The man left Woody and Amanda standing at the door. When they were walking towards the master bedroom, the man had joined a woman in the open kitchen. She was opening and closing cabinet doors.

Amanda nudged Woody. The woman was making a comment. "I like the idea of having enough space in the kitchen for a table and chairs. Plus, the pullout cabinet drawers and extra counter space are a plus. The only thing I would change is the wall paper."

Rather than go into the bedroom, Woody and Amanda eased into the kitchen. Amanda took the lead. "I love this house. I can see us living in it."

"Dear, I have to agree. There's plenty of space to entertain."

Woody re-emphasized, "I can definitely see us in this house. The crown molding and chair railing was a nice touch." He laughed. "Knowing you dear, you'll make a few changes, but overall we could move in now and make changes later."

The man turned to Woody. "I was telling my wife the very same thing. Not only that, this is the best pre-owned home we've seen today."

"How long have you been looking for a house?" Amanda asked.

The woman volunteered, "This is the third house we've looked at today."

The husband added, "Yeah, but we've been looking for weeks."

The couple told Woody and Amanda that they wanted to look at the lanai again. Woody and Amanda began whispering about how they thought the couple seemed interested.

Woody and Amanda watched as they talked to the agent in low tones. They came back inside, smiled and stopped.

The man said, "It was nice talking to you. Good luck in your house search."

When the door closed, the agent walked inside, grinning. "I told you, the house would sell quickly, but I didn't expect it to sell this fast. I've arranged to meet with the couple that just left in an hour. They want to write a contract on the house."

"What about the price?"

"They're making a full offer. I'll call you as soon as the paper work is completed. I don't want to jinx you so I won't say congratulations yet."

Excited, Woody and Amanda hugged each other. Amanda pulled away from Woody's embrace and turned to the agent.

"Thanks for everything. We can't tell you how much we appreciate all your help."

The agent laughed. "I didn't do anything. The house showed well and it sold itself. I think you should know that one of the main reasons the couple wanted to buy the house was because of the golf course view."

The End

Breinigsville, PA USA
22 March 2010
234628BV00003B/1/P